Totally Bound Publishing books by Tiffany Aaron:

Fallen Volume One
Detroit
Reno

Fallen Volume Two
New Orleans
Chicago

Fallen Volume Three
New York
Los Angeles

I0542385

FALLEN
Volume Three

New York

Los Angeles

TIFFANY AARON

Fallen Volume Three
ISBN # 978-1-78184-745-9
©Copyright Tiffany Aaron 2014
Cover Art by Posh Gosh ©Copyright 2014
Interior text design by Claire Siemaszkiewicz
Totally Bound Publishing

NEW YORK

Dedication

For those of you who fell in love with Christian and
wanted him to have his own love.

Chapter One

The lights of New York shone like small, brilliant diamonds on black velvet. Christian studied the city below him as he stood on the roof of his apartment building. So much had changed over the centuries he'd lived and the city had grown. He remembered being there when the Statue of Liberty had risen above Ellis Island. He was there the day the Twin Towers had been brought down by bad men intent on hurting innocents.

He sipped at his scotch, thinking about Chicago and what had gone on there. Seeing Lucifer face-to-face again had cracked the carefully constructed walls around Christian's sanity. The worse thing he'd seen was his own downfall reflected in Lucifer's black eyes. Over the centuries, Christian had seen his own eyes darken from bright blue to midnight blue as he'd began to lose whatever humanity he had.

Sighing, Christian shook his head. *Could angels have humanity?* Well, he was losing his sympathy for the mortals he lived amongst, and that scared him. He didn't want to become like the unrepentants he punished. Yet as hard as he fought to not fall over the edge into that abyss, it was becoming a slippery balancing act.

As he contemplated getting another drink, he felt a sudden influx of power, strong enough to almost drive him to his knees. He grimaced, knowing who had just arrived to visit him.

"Would you like a drink, Mika'il?" He didn't turn to look at the archangel, annoyed that Mika'il felt he could just come and go as he pleased.

"No. I don't know why any of you insist on drinking when it does nothing to you. You can't get drunk, so why waste the time?" Mika'il walked up beside him, then sighed. "I don't know that they'll ever get used to the new skyline."

"It's different, but within a couple of years, no one will think anything of it. Change happens, whether they are prepared for it or not." Christian held up his glass. "We drink to fit in. It is a very human activity, and we don't want to stick out amongst the crowd."

Mika'il pursed his lips, but didn't look convinced. Christian gritted his teeth, not feeling up to dealing with Mika'il at the moment.

"What do you want?" He tossed the glass into the air, and with a simple wave of his hand, made it disappear.

"Don't you want to fit in? Doing things like that stands out, Christian," the angel pointed out.

Christian shrugged. "There's no one up here to see us. I could run around naked, and no one would care."

"Heck, you could do that down on the streets, and the single thing that might happen is you'd be propositioned by someone." Mika'il chuckled. "I have to admit, that's one of the things I like about this city.

Nothing fazes people here. They go on living their lives, no matter what. It's like they won't let anything keep them down for long."

"Why are you here, Mika'il?"

"I can't come to visit one of my friends?"

Christian rolled his eyes. "You and I haven't been friends since I fell, plus you don't visit people for idle chit-chat."

"Maybe I'm starting a new practice," Mika'il commented.

"Just stop dancing around the subject and tell me what you want, Mika'il. It's going to piss me off, isn't it?" Christian clenched his hands then shoved them in the pockets of his pants.

Mika'il shifted like he was unhappy with Christian's tone. "What makes you say that?"

"You normally just show up, throw me orders then disappear. I've never seen you uneasy or uncomfortable about anything." Christian frowned. "Why didn't you show up in Chicago?"

"Couldn't. Had other things to do. Besides, you all had it under control. I knew you could handle Lucifer." Mika'il rubbed his chin then said, "I need you to check some warehouses on the river. There's been some activity around the abandoned buildings that I don't like."

Christian laughed. "There have been suspicious things happening in them since they were abandoned, Mika'il. Are you going to tell me what has you so uneasy?"

"No. Just go there, and be careful. There have been reports of some unrepentants in the area as well."

Christian snarled before saying, "There won't be any when I get done over there."

Mika'il slapped him on the shoulder. "Which is why I'm sending you instead of one of the lesser Enforcers. These particular fallen seem to be banding together and I don't like that."

With that rather cryptic statement, Mika'il disappeared, leaving Christian to wonder how unrepentants had managed to not kill each other long enough to band together. Hell, they usually tried to eliminate other fallen before going after mortals. Christian had never understood why, but Mika'il just said it was like territorial lions. They fought to protect what they consider theirs, which could be anything.

He imagined his bedroom in the penthouse below him, and a flash of power sent him there. Once he'd finished stripping, he strolled into the bathroom. He would take a shower before heading out again. Having just arrived back from Chicago, he hadn't had time to do anything except get a drink before Mika'il had shown up.

Bracing his hands against the tile of his shower, he let his head drop forward. He hated taking orders from the archangel, yet he knew he couldn't tell him no. Not after accepting the brand of an Enforcer, and turning into judge and jury against his fellow fallen.

Falling with the others wasn't the best decision I could've made. Christian grunted in annoyance. The secret most of the others didn't know was that he hadn't fallen because he'd believed in Daystar's idiotic babble about being more important than mortals. No. Christian had fallen because he believed in God's forgiveness, and wanted to prove that God loved his angels enough to forgive their rebellion.

He snatched up the soap with a sharp hiss of anger. Little had he known that there would be no forgiveness for the angels who chose to rebel in

Heaven. *He forgives mortals so easily for far worse crimes, yet He denies us the hope of returning to Heaven because we wanted to be more important to Him than mortals.*

After rinsing the lather from his body, he climbed out then turned the water off. He shoved the troubling memories of his fall to the back of his mind. While toweling down, he thought about which warehouses Mika'il meant. Christian had felt a small build-up of power rising from a group of abandoned buildings on the Hudson before he'd left for Chicago.

He paused in the middle of pulling a pair of briefs from his dresser. He'd sent Phillip down to check it out, but hadn't heard back from the other Enforcer. Once he was completely dressed, he wandered out into his living room to find his keys and wallet. While he didn't normally drive around the city, he felt the need to be out among the mortals he was supposed to protect.

As he waited in the corridor for the lift, he tugged out his phone then dialed Phillip's number. His call went to voicemail, and a hint of concern began to swell inside Christian. None of the Enforcers under him would dare miss one of his calls—he'd put the fear of him in them from the moment Mika'il had put him in charge of the entire East Coast contingent.

"Phillip, call me as soon as you can. I need to know what you found out about that power build-up." Christian ended the call.

He climbed into the lift then punched the button for the lobby. While heading down, he decided to call Samantha, another Enforcer who had been a partner of sorts to Phillip. She answered after two rings.

"Hello, sir." Nothing in her voice gave away how she felt about him calling her.

"I need to talk to Phillip. I sent him to do a job for me, and I haven't heard from him since then." Niceties were beyond him. He didn't care whether the fallen he worked with liked him or not, and his indifference had grown over the years.

He sensed a hesitation from Samantha before she replied, "I haven't seen Phillip in a week or so, sir. He seems to have disappeared shortly after you gave him his orders."

"Fuck. Did he even do what I asked him to do before then? Why didn't you contact me earlier about this?"

Christian stalked across the lobby toward the parking garage. It was one of the few places in downtown Manhattan that still had its own parking area. That was because Christian owned the property, and hadn't been willing to get rid of it. He needed a place close by to park his vehicles—it was a huge bonus for the rest of the mortals who lived in the apartment building.

"You were in Chicago, and I didn't want to bother you about it. I'm not sure, sir." She didn't call him a bastard for not being more concerned about Phillip's welfare, but Christian could tell she wanted to. "I do know that the night he vanished, he was going to head out to the docks to start looking into what you wanted."

"Hmm...and when was that?" He hit his key fob to unlock his car, then slid behind the wheel. He didn't start the engine, wanting to finish his conversation with Samantha before going anywhere.

"I believe it was the same night you ordered him to go look, sir." Again there was no inflection in her voice, but for some reason, Christian had the feeling that she blamed him for Phillip being gone.

"All right. Did Phillip say anything to you before he left?"

"Not that I can remember, sir."

Christian frowned, then said, "If you can think of anything he might have said before he headed out, let me know." He hung up then tossed his phone onto the seat next to him.

Phillip missing didn't sound promising, and while Christian didn't care one way or another whether Phillip was around or not, he did want to know if Phillip was taken or if he chose to leave. Of course, if he'd left, Phillip was supposed to have told Christian that he was going.

"You don't believe he took off," Christian muttered aloud as he started the car.

After pulling out of the underground parking garage, he turned in the direction of the docks. Something had happened to Phillip, and Christian had the feeling it had to do with the unrepentants. The less powerful Enforcer was scared of Christian, and he wouldn't go anywhere outside the city without Christian's permission.

The closer he got to the abandoned warehouses along the river, the more oppressive the atmosphere became. Christian curled his upper lip in a snarl at unrepentants who thought they could get away with gathering in his territory.

Yet it was unusual to have so many fallen in one spot. The fallen who had gone over the edge tended to become solitary as they hunted among the mortals. Paranoia grew as the madness did until they would try to kill each other.

Could Lucifer have anything to do with the gathering? If so, what was Lucifer up to? Was he finally planning to take over the world starting with New York?

Christian frowned as he pulled up in front of one of the empty buildings. Fallen had been there, but they had either left or moved on because the skin-crawling feeling he normally associated with them wasn't nearly as bad as it had been elsewhere. He climbed from the car then stretched while studying the area around him.

The stench of garbage and unwashed bodies filled his nostrils and he fought back the urge to gag. More than fallen called this place home, which didn't surprise Christian that much. The homeless on the streets of New York City needed to find places to spend the cold winter nights. They also needed to find places to hide when the police came to roust them out of the parks.

He'd lived in the city long enough to have seen the increase in the street people who called abandoned places like this home, and had lost his compassion for them. Christian didn't understand why they didn't make their own lives better by finding jobs and homes. It wasn't that complicated to choose *not* to live like this.

"Hey, honey, you looking for some company?"

Turning around, he barely managed to keep the disgust from showing on his face. The girl couldn't have been any older than nineteen or twenty. Her ragged, dirty clothes barely covered the most private parts of her body. Even though she stood in a shadowed alley a few feet from him, Christian could see her clearly, and he shuddered.

The whore was skinny to the point of starvation, the bones in her wrists and hips sticking out. The scabs on her arms and legs told him her story. Another mortal who had lost her battle with heroin, and had decided the drug was better than anything else in her life. She would give him a blowjob or let him fuck her for the money she needed for her next fix.

Christian no longer cared why they chose to numb their lives with drugs. Why getting lost in the haze of heroin or meth made their lives better, he didn't understand, and no longer wanted to.

"I'm not interested," he said, looking away from her to study the building again.

"Come on, mister. I'll make it worth your time."

"Shouldn't you be making it worth my money?"

Why are you talking to her? Just get the job done and get the hell home.

He sensed her confusion at his question, but before he could clarify it, and maybe see if she had any brain cells left, three people came walking down the sidewalk. Christian looked them over, but since they were only human, he didn't have anything to worry from them. He started to make his way toward the warehouse.

"Mindy, are you okay?"

Something about the voice that spoke the gentle question froze Christian in his tracks. His heart skipped a beat, and his cock hardened in a way that it hadn't in years. Every atom in his body was on alert to hear more of that voice.

Whirling around, he found the trio standing next to the alleyway, and the male of the group glared at him in an attempt to scare him while the two women talked to the whore. Totally unconcerned about the man, Christian strolled over to where they were gathered.

"Who are you?" he asked.

The women turned to look at him. The guy was tall and muscular, obviously there for protection. The woman was short and curvy with short blonde hair and bright blue eyes. As big as the guy was, Christian got the feeling he needed to worry more about this petite female.

The taller brunette didn't glance at him as she kept her attention on Mindy. Christian had never liked being ignored, and for some reason it was worse when this woman did it.

"I'm fine, Joan. Just chatting with that fellow. Trying to work out a price."

Christian huffed in annoyance. "We weren't working out a price. I have never paid for sex, and I'm not about to now."

The blonde didn't look convinced, and the man rolled his eyes, probably having heard it all before. Christian found himself wanting to protest that he was telling the truth. Having to explain himself wasn't something he'd ever done, not really caring what any mortal thought of him, but the urge to elaborate on his presence on that sidewalk caught him off guard.

"Joan, why don't you talk to Mindy and give her the stuff we brought for her? I want to chat with Mr Tall, Blond and Stuck-Up over here."

Watching as Joan led Mindy a few steps down the alley, Christian then whirled to meet the other woman's gaze. "What exactly did you want to talk to me about?"

"You should really watch your tone, Mister. It doesn't take any more time to be nice than it does to be an asshole." The guy crossed his arms over his chest and stared at Christian.

"Did you just make that up? Do you read fortune cookies for fun or something?" Christian clenched his teeth in annoyance. "I have things to get done, and you're wasting my time."

He started to turn around and walk away, but the blonde put her hand on his arm, and short of shoving her away, he couldn't do anything. While he might not like mortals much anymore, he wasn't going to go around assaulting them either.

"What's a guy like you doing down here if you're not looking for a little sex?" She tilted her head in the direction of Mindy and Joan. "I'm Cecila, by the way, and this is Piet."

Did he look like he cared what their names were?

A sudden wave of uneasiness swept over him, and Christian knew a fallen was near. He set his feet and spread his awareness out a little thicker, trying to figure out exactly where the creature was.

"A polite person would introduce himself and answer my question, especially if he wasn't doing anything illegal." Cecila propped her fists on her hips and studied him with a narrow-eyed glare.

"I'm sure that look works on people who have had mothers to make them feel guilty, but I haven't, so it won't work on me." Christian gestured toward the warehouse behind them. "I came to look at that place."

There wasn't any point in not telling them what he was doing. In fact, if they were down near the docks a lot, they might know something about the unrepentants.

Piet curled his upper lip. "Looking for investment properties?"

Christian shook his head. "I'm interested in a group of people that had been seen hanging around the warehouses. Have you seen them?"

Cecila shrugged. "We see a lot of people while doing our job. Are they prostitutes or junkies? Homeless? You aren't going to have them arrested, are you? That's not a very charitable thing to do."

Frowning, Christian studied the older woman. "Do I strike you as a man who does charity work or who even cares about charity?"

"No." Piet didn't hesitate.

"And you know why?" He paused, but when there wasn't anything forthcoming, he continued, "Because I'm not."

"Harsh."

Joan's comment caused Christian to look up to see Joan walking up to join them. Mindy was nowhere to be seen, yet the other presence Christian had felt was still around, watching them. He turned in a three-sixty circle, looking for anything that was out of place and feeling for empty spots in the energies surrounding them. He couldn't sense anyone else, but that didn't mean anything. Fallen could hide from him if they tried, or if they banded their power together.

"What are you doing?" Joan asked once he faced them again.

"Just checking to make sure no one is getting close." Christian tugged back his cuff to check his watch. "I need to go, but if you could answer my question? Have you seen a group of people gathering in one of these buildings? They might look like they're homeless, junkies or whores, but they're something else all together."

"What are they?" Piet inquired, but Christian wasn't interested in talking any more.

"Have you seen them?" he demanded.

"Actually, yes. A few days ago, there were about ten strangers hanging around warehouse fourteen. It's three blocks west of here." Joan motioned behind Christian. "I saw them when I was out giving the working girls some condoms."

"Is that what you do down here? Give the whores condoms?" Christian scowled. "Don't you know how dangerous that is?"

"We're well aware of the danger, Mr...?" Joan let her voice fade out.

Christian wasn't going to be drawn into revealing his name. As attracted as he was to Joan, it didn't mean he was going to spill all of his personal information to people he didn't know.

"I suggest you rethink your little charity handouts for a few weeks, or go somewhere else in this God-forsaken city. That group is far more deadly than your usual whores and druggies."

Joan and Piet snorted.

"What?"

"It's obvious you don't come down to the mean streets very often," Cecila commented, staring pointedly at the Rolex on his wrist and his Jaguar F-Type S parked at the curb. "Have you ever been down on your luck and needing help from someone? Have you ever lived the hell on earth that a lot people living on the street experience every day?"

Anger surging through him, Christian pushed into Cecila's personal space. She gasped when she met his gaze, and Christian imagined his eyes were almost black with his dark emotions.

"I live in hell every day of my life, lady, and I've lived far longer than you or anyone else on the streets of this city. I've experienced unimaginable pain, so don't judge me like you know me." Christian snarled.

"All right, sir. Just back up. Cecila didn't mean anything by it." Joan rested her hand on Christian's arm, encouraging him to move.

Even though there were two layers of clothes between his skin and hers, Christian swore he could feel the smoothness of her fingers. Of course, that wasn't true, but he could imagine how her touch would feel on his body. He grunted as his cock hardened again.

He shifted away from her, not wanting her to know how much she'd affected him. It had been over a year since he'd been interested enough in a woman to take her to bed. What was it about Joan that caught his attention?

Her brunette hair was long and bound at her nape by a small blue ribbon. He met her wide hazel eyes with his own, not wanting to give anything away. Yet her sharp inhale told him she must have seen some of what he was feeling.

She stepped back at the same time as he did, then she cleared her throat. "They were there for a night or two before they left. I haven't seen as large a group again. I have seen two or three together at a time, coming and going from the same building."

"Thank you." He took another step away from her, thinking it probably looked as if he was scared to death of her. It was just that he didn't have time to deal with this strange need he felt for her. "I suggest if you're going to continue the foolish campaign of helping out the destitute then you should go somewhere else for a little while."

"You really don't care for those less fortunate than you, do you?" Joan's question was so soft, Christian had to lean closer to hear it.

Rearing back, he took a deep breath as shock raced through him.

"Where has your compassion gone, Christian?" Mika'il's voice echoed his own thoughts. *"At one time, you were no better than those you sneer at."*

"Keep them safe, Piet, and listen to me. Stay away from these warehouses for a little while. There are far more dangerous things in the world then an angry pimp or a strung-out junkie."

After turning, he stalked over to his car. To hell with looking for the fallen tonight. He'd go home and lick his wounds, then come back tomorrow when there wouldn't be any mortals to bother him.

"Wait. Please."

He froze where he stood by the car door. Shooting a glance over his shoulder, he saw Joan jogging toward him. "Yes?"

"What's your name?"

Christian hadn't intended to tell her because he thought she didn't need to know. At that moment, it was like someone else had taken over his tongue. "Christian Vosberg," he muttered.

She held out her hand. "I'm Joan Fisher. It's nice to meet you, Mr Vosberg. Maybe we'll see each other again."

He shook her hand. "Maybe we will, Ms Fisher."

He let go of her hand before sliding behind the wheel, then starting the engine. He barely stopped himself from slamming on the gas pedal to peel away from the curb. Not wanting Joan to know she bothered him, Christian eased away from the sidewalk then headed out of the city. It was time to get away, clear his head and refocus on his job. Yet he looked into the rear view mirror to see Joan standing at the curb, staring after him. Something told him he wouldn't be forgetting her anytime soon.

Chapter Two

Joan flopped into the chair closest to the door, not trying to stop it as it scooted across the floor on its wheels. She didn't really react when it hit the wall behind her.

"I'm beat," she commented as Cecila and Piet joined her in the office. After checking the clock on the wall, she sighed. It was four in the morning, and all she really wanted to do was go home and crash for a couple of hours before she had to go into work.

"So am I, but thank you both for going with me." Cecila smiled at them. "It's safer to have more than one person with you."

"Which is why I tell you to call me when you're going out," Piet spoke up. He leaned against Cecila's desk and grinned. "The ladies might not have a problem with you stopping by, but their pimps and the junkies who think you have something to steal do."

"I know." Joan tugged the band out of her hair then shook out the curls. "When I found out where Cecila wanted to go, I called you. Mr Vosberg's right. That group I saw at the warehouses aren't the kind anyone wants to mess with."

Cecila moved behind the desk to take her seat. "I think Vosberg is another one you shouldn't mess with."

"He was an ass."

Joan had to agree with Piet's assessment of Christian Vosberg, yet she remembered the lust she'd seen when he'd looked at her. But more than that, it was the anguish she'd heard in his voice and had seen in his dark blue eyes when he'd yelled at Cecila, that wouldn't leave her mind.

"True, but I think there's more to him than we saw. He did warn us to stay away from the warehouses," she couldn't help but point out.

Cecila frowned and Piet simply stayed quiet. Joan had a feeling Christian hadn't impressed either of them. Of course, he hadn't been very compassionate toward the prostitutes, junkies and homeless they'd gone out to help. They'd run across a lot of folks like that, who thought they were better than those living on the street because they had a job, a home or food to eat. They didn't see that at some point the very people they looked down on had once had all of those things as well. Then something happened, and life turned to shit.

Joan had lived on the streets four years ago, an alcoholic and a step away from selling her body for a drink. Just as she'd hit rock bottom, someone had offered her a helping hand, and she'd taken it instead of being too proud to accept it.

"Why do you think he was there?" She spoke aloud, though she knew her friends didn't know.

Piet shrugged. "Who knows? Probably scoping the buildings out to remodel into condos or something like that."

The scorn in her best friend's voice surprised Joan. "Do you have something against him having money? Though we shouldn't just assume that he does."

Cecila snorted so loudly, both Joan and Piet stared at her. She waved her hand in a vague, dismissive gesture.

"I'm sure he's barely surviving, and that the Rolex and Jaguar are just something he borrows from his best friend when he wants to impress the ladies." She shook her head. "No, honey. That man has money. Probably more than we'll ever have in our entire lives combined."

"Right. Come on. Are you telling me you've never heard of Christian Vosberg before?" Piet tugged his phone out, then started doing something on it.

"No, I haven't. I assume you know who he is." Joan laughed. "I don't have a TV. Too busy working, going to school and helping you out."

"But you could keep up on the news using your laptop," Piet pointed out.

She could, but Joan had decided she wasn't going to spend her time on the net checking gossip sites and stuff like that. Keeping up with her classes and work was more difficult than she'd thought it would be. Of course, going back to college at thirty didn't help either.

"I don't have time to keep up on the society pages, jackass. Just tell me who he is already." Joan poked Piet in the side after he moved to stand next to her. She took the phone from him.

"Christian Vosberg is one of the richest and most powerful men in the city. No one knows how much real estate he owns around the world."

Joan read everything that was on Christian's Wikipedia page, though she wasn't sure how much she should believe. But even if half of it wasn't true, the rest overwhelmed her.

"And this guy was down by the docks, about to go into an abandoned warehouse by himself?" She handed the phone back and frowned. "Where were his bodyguards or entourage? Most guys with that much money have a lot of hangers-on."

Cecila bit her bottom lip as she seemed to be thinking. Piet shoved his hands in his pockets.

"The weird thing is he's always alone. He doesn't have bodyguards or security people. If he goes to any events, he's usually alone. I've never seen him with a woman. Maybe he's gay."

Joan remembered the desire burning in Christian's eyes when he looked at her right before he climbed in his car. She shuddered as her own lust overtook her. Shifting in her chair, she giggled. "Trust me. He isn't gay."

The knowing look she got from Cecila caused her to blush, and Joan ducked her head, but she couldn't get rid of the smile on her face. Joan had been so focused on getting her life back on track that it had been a long time since she'd been attracted to a man.

Now that she had, maybe she was ready to start dating or at least checking gorgeous men out when she ran across them. Not that she met many gorgeous, eligible men during the course of her day. When she wasn't working, she was in school or roaming the streets to help out the people who found themselves there. Her busy schedule wasn't conducive to dating.

Christian's dark blue eyes flashed through her mind and Joan flushed again. If she secretly hoped to see Christian again, no one else needed to know. She might have some nice dreams when she slept, too.

"Do you think he's looking to buy some property? If he was, then why did he ask about that group of people we saw down there? Vosberg seemed to be far more interested in them than the building," Cecila pointed out.

"You said you saw them, Joan. Did they accost you or something? You know I hate you going out there by yourself." Piet glared at her.

She shrugged. "I was taking some condoms to Mindy and the girls. You weren't around, and I knew they were running out. We're doing a good thing, helping them stay clean of STDs and pregnancies at least, even if we can't keep them off the drugs or get them out of their profession."

Neither of her friends were going to argue with her about that, though Joan understood their fear about her going on her own. The places they went weren't the safest in the city, and there were some people who'd just as soon kill her as look at her. Joan accepted that she might die one night, killed by a druggie or a pimp, but she wasn't going to worry about it. If it happened, it happened, and she would count herself lucky that she'd been able to help people out before she died.

"I have to admit I didn't really study them that closely, and they didn't react to me in any way." Joan paused as she thought about the actions of the group she'd seen earlier that week. "You know, that seems weird to me. They truly didn't react to me, not even to look at me. It was like I wasn't even there."

"What were they doing?"

She shrugged. "Nothing that I could see, though to be honest, there were ten of them outside the building when I got there. I think there were probably more inside the warehouse, but I didn't see any of the others. I do know that the homeless haven't slept in the area of those particular buildings for over a week or so. Tonight was the first time I saw any of the working girls around there as well."

"Much like animals, those who live on the streets can sense danger and will avoid places where it might lurk. So if they're returning to the area, then whoever those people are, they must have moved on." Piet checked his watch then yawned. "I need to head home and grab some sleep. You ladies make sure to text me when you get back to your places."

They agreed, and he hugged each of them before he left. Cecila gestured to the open door. "Why don't you head home as well, Joan? I have some paperwork to fill out, then file before I get to go."

Stretching, Joan nodded. "Yeah. I don't have classes today, but I do have to go into work at six, so I should probably get some rest."

She gave the older lady a quick hug before leaving the office. After grabbing her bag from one of the lockers in the break room, Joan headed out into the early morning to flag down a cab. She was on her way home in a few minutes.

Leaning her head back against the seat in the cab, Joan closed her eyes and took a deep breath. As she cleared her mind, a sudden image of Christian Vosberg drifted through and she shifted uncomfortably as her thighs clenched with desire.

Tall, blond and gorgeous, Christian had an intriguing air of sadness hanging over him. Joan couldn't help but wonder what Christian had to be sad about. From all accounts, or at least what Piet had told her, he had more money than God, and owned more of the city than the mayor. Yet there was something that made her think he was just biding his time or balancing on the edge of some kind of meltdown.

She thought about the emotion in his voice when he'd told Cecila, "*I live in hell every day of my life, lady, and I've lived far longer than you or anyone else on the streets of this city. I've experienced unimaginable pain, so don't judge me like you know me.*"

Just remembering the agony coloring his words brought tears to her eyes. What could have happened to Christian to make him feel like that? She could probably find out if she went online and did a search for him, but for some reason, she didn't like the idea of prying into his private life.

Joan chuckled, knowing it didn't matter whether she did or didn't. She wasn't ever going to see Christian again, so why would she waste time she didn't have in reading gossip about the man?

The cab driver rolled to a stop at the curb in front of Joan's apartment building. After paying him, she made her way up to her apartment. She stripped then took a quick shower. She hoped to get enough sleep to be able to function when she got into work later that day.

As she curled up under the blankets, Joan let her mind drift back to Christian Vosberg, and what she'd felt when she'd encountered him. It was nice to know she could feel those emotions again. After her long journey to getting sober, she hadn't thought she'd be able to find any man attractive as she straightened her life out. Working a full time job and going back school filled her days so she simply didn't have the time to flirt or even look for company.

Christian was handsome and rich. Two things that took him out of Joan's world and set him in his own, where they wouldn't meet again. It was a rare confluence of events that had brought them together. Joan appreciated it, but she knew better than to hope it would happen again.

As she drifted off to sleep, Christian's image stayed in her mind, and she slept with a smile on her face.

* * * *

The bell rang over the door of the diner as someone walked in. Joan looked up from where she stood behind the counter, chatting with one of the late dinner crowd. She smiled as she spotted the familiar blond gentleman making his way to a booth in her section. After grabbing the coffee pot, she walked over to him.

"I thought I wouldn't be seeing you any more now that I've straightened my life out," she said while flipping over a mug, then filling it with coffee.

Lucian chuckled and she was struck by how even that sounded like church bells on a clear day. "I have a vested interest in making sure you stay sober. Besides, I'm not the type of guy who dumps friends when things change."

Joan covered Lucian's hand closest to her. "I really do appreciate everything you did for me while I hit bottom. Not many of my friends stuck around."

His black eyes shone with understanding, and Lucian's smile held a little bit of sadness. "I know what it's like to lose all your friends, even those you considered family."

"You want your usual?" She knew better than to ask him what his comment meant. One thing that Lucian had never done before was explain himself. She didn't know anything more about his personal life than she had when they'd first met seven years ago.

He nodded, and she left to place his order. After checking on her other customers, Joan wandered back to where Lucian sat. She studied his face, never lingering on the cross-shaped brand on his left cheek. So many times she'd bit her tongue to stop from asking about it, sure it had something to do with the occasional sadness and weariness she'd seen on his face and heard in his voice.

Yet there was something about him tonight, and she frowned as she tried to work out what was bothering her.

"Did you and the group have a good night? Hand out all the condoms and needles you had?" Lucian sipped his coffee and looked at her with a straightforward expression.

"Yes. Managed to grab some sleep before I came into work. We'll probably go back out tomorrow night." She fidgeted as she thought about Christian Vosberg, then it hit her and she gasped.

"What?" Lucian lowered his pale eyebrows and frowned at her.

"I met someone tonight who could've been your twin," she informed her friend. "Only he had dark blue eyes, not black. I've been meaning to ask you, how in the hell do you have black eyes like that? There's no pupils or anything. It's like staring into the endless expanse of space without stars."

Lucian dropped his gaze to the cup in his hands, and she wondered if he was going to answer her question.

His shoulders lifted then dropped as he took a deep breath before exhaling.

"It's a rare medical condition. I see fine, but for some reason there's no definition to my pupils." He cleared his throat. "What was this handsome man's name?"

"Christian Vosberg. I guess he's some kind of multi-millionaire or something. I'd never heard of him until last night." She narrowed her eyes. "How did you know he was handsome?"

Lucian gestured toward his own face. "You said he looked like me, so of course he has to be good-looking."

There was something in his tone that she didn't believe. Almost as if he was lying about something, yet she couldn't imagine why. So she let it go because she considered herself lucky that Lucian chose to talk to her at all.

"So you've heard of Christian Vosberg?"

"Yes, I know Vosberg. We've had a few business dealings." He shrugged. "You can't do anything in this city without running into him."

Joan wondered at the hint of bitterness in her friend's voice. Maybe Christian had beaten Lucian at some business deal or something.

"How ever did you run across him? You must admit you don't really run in the same circles. He's not the type to go slumming."

She glared at him. "Thanks a lot. Are you saying he's too good for me?"

"No, honey. I'm simply saying that Christian Vosberg rarely comes out of his ivory tower long enough to mingle with the common folk."

Standing, Joan stared at Lucian's Versace suit. "He's not the only one who doesn't lower himself to see how regular people live."

She made the rounds of her tables, filling mugs, cashing out bills and delivering food. After making sure everyone else was happy, Joan returned to Lucian's booth, bringing his meal with her.

"It's true that I don't often find a need to dirty my hands by interacting with people." There was a slight sneer on his face when he said 'people', like he thought it was a disgusting word, or maybe it was the people themselves he didn't care for.

Joan had always known Lucian had money, but she'd never asked about how he made it. For the most part, during their friendship, she'd been so caught up in her own situation, she'd never gone out of her way to talk to Lucian about his own life. As arrogant and snobby as he was, Lucian had been there for her while she'd struggled against her addiction. He'd been merciless in denying her that which she wanted so badly.

"Why did you help me?" She'd asked the same question of him since they'd met.

He studied his half-empty plate. "You puzzled me, and I wanted to solve you."

"Solve me? Like I'm a Rubik's Cube or something?" She propped her fists on her hips as she asked.

Squinting at her, he pursed his lips for a second while he seemed to be thinking about something. "What's a Rubik's Cube?"

"Never mind. I guess I shouldn't get upset at whatever caused you to help me." She took his money, knowing he gave her enough for the bill and a nice sized tip. Joan moved back as he stood.

"I was glad to help you, Joan. You're a good person, and I haven't run into many of them in my life." He leaned down, then brushed a kiss over her cheek. "One word of advice though. I'd stay away from

Vosberg. He's not the type of man a woman like you should be involved with."

Before she could ask what he meant by that, Lucian was gone, and she was left wondering what kind of bad blood existed between her friend and Christian. Joan took care of Lucian's plates, then went on to finish the rest of her shift.

Chapter Three

Christian settled behind his desk, but didn't look at the papers in front of him. He stared across his office at the wall while he tried to get Joan out of his mind. It had been three days since he'd met the woman, yet he'd thought about her several times during the hours he was awake. He shifted in his chair when he remembered several graphic dreams he'd had about Joan as well.

"I need to stop thinking about her. I'm not ever going to see her again," he muttered, scrubbing his hands over his face. "It's not like I don't have other things to worry about."

"Talking to yourself isn't a good sign." Mika'il suddenly materialized in the room.

He did his best not to react to Mika'il appearing out of nowhere. "I was talking to the only person whose opinion I trust."

Mika'il chuckled. "Right. You do seem to be distracted, which isn't usual. I wonder what has you so worked up that you're talking to yourself?"

"It's nothing," Christian answered, not wanting Mika'il to know about Joan. The archangel would tease him unmercifully if he realized Christian couldn't seem to forget about Joan.

"Sure." Mika'il didn't sound convinced, but seemed to be willing to let it go. "Did you learn anything about why the unrepentants were gathering at that warehouse?"

"Not yet. The Enforcer I sent to check it out has disappeared."

Mika'il tensed. "Do you think he was killed or could he have run away?"

"That's the thing. Phillip wouldn't have run off. If he wanted to leave, he would've said something to me about it. He fears me, and he knows that I wouldn't be happy if he were to just disappear." Christian stood then walked over to the window, but he didn't see the skyline beyond the glass. "Are you telling me you don't know what happened to him? I thought you could keep track of all of us."

The archangel frowned. "It's not that I've lost track of Phillip, but there's an emptiness in the place where his presence used to be."

Christian wasn't sure what Mika'il meant, but he didn't want to ask. It had always been enough for him that Mika'il was able to track him wherever he went, like some kind of Heavenly version of GPS. Yet now Mika'il seemed to be saying he could lose track of fallen, and Christian liked that idea even less than Mika'il knowing where he was at every minute of the day.

"When did you lose him?" Christian asked.

"A day or two after you left." Mika'il stuffed his hands in his pockets, wrinkling his suit and broadcasting his worry. "I was too caught up in what was going on in Chicago to focus on his disappearance. I figured I'd look into it after the situation was fixed."

Christian nodded. "That's around the same time that Samantha said she'd lost touch with Phillip as well. I guess I need to find the unrepentants that were using those particular warehouses."

He was pretty sure that was what Mika'il had wanted from the beginning, but he'd never spent his life blindly following what the archangel said. So he'd tried to get someone else to do the work for him.

"Yes, you need to be the one who does it. None of the other Enforcers have the strength to fight off a coordinated attack by several unrepentants." Mika'il cleared his throat. "I think Lucifer is in town."

Christian wasn't worried about Daystar. "He often comes here. There's a lot of greed, corruption and violence here. He can absorb a great deal of power from being in New York for an hour."

"True. Just be careful. He goes out of his way to search you out and tries to upset you." Mika'il studied him.

"Are you surprised by that? He was like that before any of us fell. I think it's in his nature to annoy and irritate everyone he possibly can."

Mika'il's grunt sounded as if he agreed. "All right. I'll let you get to work on solving this unrepentant problem. We can't have them joining forces, Christian. You know how bad that could end up being, for mortals and for us."

"Of course I know, Mika'il. Why do you think I've been doing this for centuries? Lucifer could do some serious damage if he gets them to combine their powers." Christian rubbed his neck. "I just don't know how to keep them from doing this besides draining them of power, and that doesn't seem very fair."

"Fair? These are fallen who have turned away from the Father and the purpose they were created for. They chose this. God didn't start out banishing them from Heaven. It was their choice to rebel." Mika'il threw his hands up in the air.

Christian turned back to face the window as he remembered the rebellion and how shocked he'd been at the number of angels that had followed Lucifer. What had convinced them that Lucifer knew what he was talking about? Why did they believe that rebelling against God was the best way to get him to pay attention to them?

And how foolish was he to choose to fall to prove how forgiving God was? He should've known it wouldn't be that easy. He'd never believed angels should be equal to God, or even equal to the mortals God loved. Christian had never cared because he'd been doing what he was created to do—obey God's commands in all things.

Yet in a moment of sheer idiocy, he'd decided to prove something by going with his brethren when they were banished from Heaven. Christian had been so certain God wouldn't turn his back on them. When he asked God to forgive him for leaving, he'd found out God wasn't inclined to be forgiving, and his heart had broken.

"Yes, it was their choice to rebel, but to force them to always stay solitary for the rest of their long lives... In a way, I'm not surprised they go insane," he muttered.

Mika'il huffed in annoyance, but he didn't comment on Christian's statement. "Just do what I tell you, Christian. Find out where and why these unrepentants are gathering. I want to make sure they're not planning something, so that we can be ready."

As much as he wanted to ask if God had said anything about what might be coming, Christian bit his tongue. Mika'il wouldn't have told him if the archangel truly knew what was going on.

"Yes, sir. I'll do that and get back to you. I need to find out what happened to Phillip as well."

"Good." Mika'il slapped him on the shoulder, then disappeared in a soft flash of light.

Once he was gone, Christian sighed as he walked into his bedroom. It was time to do some work, and while it wasn't going to be something he enjoyed, he knew he didn't have a choice. Pulling out a T-shirt and jeans, he made plans to start searching the city for the unrepentants.

"Samantha, meet me at Washington Square. We need to talk."

"Yes, sir." Samantha's reply was prompt and held a hint of worry.

"You aren't in trouble. I need to discuss Phillip and the unrepentants with you."

He didn't have any interest in dealing with her worry about what he was going to do to her. He knew his reputation had become such that no one wanted to deal with him, and for the most part, he was fine with that. Their opinions didn't matter to him, because he wasn't looking for friends or relationships.

"All right. I'll head there right now." Samantha sounded only a little reassured.

"Thank you."

Samantha's surprise at his thanks rolled through him. Christian closed his mind to her, then grinned. It was always nice to do something unexpected, and keep everyone on their toes.

He finished dressing, and since he didn't feel like driving through city traffic, he closed his eyes and thought about Washington Square. A surge of power rushed through him as he dissolved from where he stood in his penthouse.

A wall of noise slammed into him as he materialized on the corner of the square. Christian kept hidden for a moment, wanting to make sure no one was paying attention to him when he appeared. It was best if mortals didn't notice him popping up out of thin air. Of course, most of them would dismiss it as something that hadn't happened. It was their mind playing tricks on them.

"Hello, sir."

Turning, he spotted Samantha leaning against a building a few feet away. He nodded at her while gesturing toward a nearby coffee shop.

"Why don't we go in and sit? We need to talk about Phillip, and I also need you to do a little bit of investigating for me as well."

"Certainly." She led the way into the shop then joined the line at the counter.

They waited until they were seated in the corner. Christian sat with his back to the wall, keeping his eyes on the mortals in the room in front of him. Samantha didn't say anything, just sipped her coffee while Christian worked out what to say.

"I'm afraid that Phillip might have been killed by the unrepentants."

She inhaled sharply and sadness flashed in her eyes, but she didn't try to refute him. "I'm not surprised. It's not like him not to stay in touch, even when he was doing a job for you."

Christian nodded. "I know that, which is why I do believe we have a problem. If it was just one unrepentant, Phillip should've been able to deal with it without our help. He's trained and knows how to handle himself."

"Which makes you think he was attacked by more than one of them?" Samantha shifted in her chair, seemingly uncomfortable with the idea of unrepentants hanging out together. "But them being together changes the dynamics of things."

"Right. What I'd want you to do is try and find out what—if anything—Phillip discovered before he disappeared. See if you can figure out who he talked to and what they had to say." Christian ran his finger around the edge of his coffee mug. "I'll see if I can find any warehouses or abandoned buildings where they might be gathering again. This can't be allowed to happen, and all of us will have to keep a lookout, in case this is a new phenomena."

Samantha met his gaze, which wasn't something that happened very often. "What does the archangel have to say about this?"

"Just that we need to find out why the unrepentants are hanging around each other. He didn't say whether he knows what's happening or not. Mika'il isn't inclined to share his secrets with us." Christian shrugged. "He isn't inclined to share much of anything with us."

"Why would he? If we aren't worthy enough to be allowed back into Heaven, then we aren't worthy enough to share in the thoughts of God and his obedient servants."

He agreed with what Samantha said, but it didn't lessen his irritation at Mika'il withholding information that would make Christian's life easier. Of course, being annoyed didn't mean Mika'il would change his ways. So many times when the archangel had ordered him to do something, Christian had a feeling there was another reason besides the obvious one behind it.

Mika'il had another agenda that he was working along with trying to keep the unrepentants from hurting mortals, but Christian hadn't been able to figure out what it was yet.

"I'll head out and start asking around, plus I'll pass the word along to the others about keeping an eye out." Samantha stood then bowed to Christian. "I'll get back to you in a few days. Sooner if I find anything out."

"Good. And I'll let you know if I find anything worth noting. I'm going to start looking through the warehouses and places where they might meet up without being noticed."

"If you feel the need for backup, contact me, sir."

"I will."

He watched the Enforcer stroll from the café, but his mind wasn't on her. For some reason it had gone back to Joan, and his body's reaction to the mortal. Having focused so much of his energy on staying sane, he hadn't been interested in sex or a relationship with someone.

Well, not that he'd ever been interested in a relationship. Falling in love wasn't possible for an Enforcer, or so he'd thought until Chicago and meeting all those couples. While he hadn't been thrilled to be there, he had found it interesting to see them together, and know that at least for those four couples, love worked.

What would it be like to come home every night to Joan? Knowing the brunette beauty was waiting for him? What would it feel like to press his lips to hers, and taste her skin?

Obnoxiously loud laughter shook him out of his contemplation, and Christian finished his coffee before he left. He couldn't keep thinking about Joan, especially since he wasn't ever going to see her again.

He strolled out of the coffee house then paused as he thought about where to go look first. At the moment, he wasn't getting any concentrated grouping of tainted power from the unrepentants. There were hundreds of the fallen throughout the city, but he ignored them as long as they weren't bothering mortals.

Had they found out he was searching for them and hidden away? Or had that gathering just been a rare situation and they weren't ever going to do it again?

Christian couldn't help but hope it was just a one-time thing, and it wasn't a new plot by Lucifer to get more power or consolidate what he had. He couldn't very well contact Daystar and ask him. Christian couldn't trust any answer Lucifer would give him.

Sighing, he decided to return to the warehouse he'd been going to look at when he'd met Joan. It was the one place where he knew for sure the unrepentants had been together. He'd meant to go back sooner, but had gotten sidetracked with his mortal businesses. Maybe he could find someone, other than Joan, who could give him some more information about them.

"If you don't, you will have to go talk to this Joan woman again." Mika'il's voice entered his mind, and Christian frowned.

"I'm sure I won't need to talk to her again." He didn't want to because of his attraction to Joan—it was too raw and visceral for him to be comfortable around her.

43

"*Why don't you want to talk to her? I've never known you to be afraid of a woman before.*" There was a hint of teasing in Mika'il's voice.

"*I'm not afraid of her,*" Christian protested. "*I just don't see why I need to involve her in this. We know that if Lucifer is part of this, he'll find some way to reel her in.*"

"*Pure souls are the most attractive to Daystar, but we can't protect her from him. Especially if she has information we need to keep millions safe. Unfortunately, the life of one can be sacrificed for the lives of many.*"

Christian hated the fact that Mika'il was right. He understood, but it didn't mean he liked the idea of throwing Joan to the lions, or Lucifer, who could be worse than any predator.

"*I know,*" he agreed. "*I'll see what I can find, and see what Samantha discovers, but if I must, I'll go and talk to Joan.*"

"*Good.*"

He felt an emptiness in his brain when Mika'il left. After that, Christian thought about the warehouse he'd been at, and in a surge of power, he dematerialized from the street.

When he next appeared, he was standing in front of the abandoned warehouse he'd been going to the other night. Christian looked around as he stretched, testing the level of his power he had left.

When Christian was younger, he'd had to have sex with women to replenish his power, but as he'd gotten older, he'd realized all he needed to do was meditate, and it would build back up. He heard footsteps approaching from the alleyway.

"You're back."

He whirled around to see Joan standing there. *Shit!* After all that talk about avoiding her and never seeing her again, there she stood. He took a deep breath and his groin tightened when her fresh scent hit his nose.

"I didn't get a chance to look over the property," he said, shifting to try to find a little more room in his jeans.

Joan smiled. "Are you sure you're not here to try and find Mindy again?"

Christian frowned as he tried to place the name. "Mindy? Who is that?"

"The prostitute you were talking to when we showed up the other night," Joan reminded him.

"Oh." He shook his head. "I don't remember her. I really am here to look at the building. I'm not interested in whores."

Joan opened her mouth, and he figured she was going to protest about him calling Mindy a whore. He held up his hand to stop her.

"I'm not going to argue semantics with you. Whore and prostitute are just words, and it really doesn't change what she does for a living." He shrugged. "I don't care one way or the other what she does to make money, though I don't think selling her body here on these corners will help her pay her rent."

Her abrupt laugh surprised him, and Christian met her hazel eyes, seeing amusement there. He raised his eyebrows in question.

"Any money she makes goes to her pimp, and she shares a room with three other ladies. Do you truly think she should move up in the world, and find a corner that will make her more money? Her pimp tells her where to go." Joan wrapped her arms around her waist as she glanced around.

"There isn't anyone else besides us here. You don't have to worry about being seen talking to me. If that was what you were worried about," he qualified.

She shook her head. "I'm not worried about being seen talking to you. Hell, I'm not a working girl. I just hate being around here, especially lately."

"What are you talking about?" He eased some of his power out to the space around them, testing the atmosphere.

Joan inched closer to him, and Christian fought the urge to embrace her. He had to stay away from her. It was bad enough he was going to have to bring her into the investigation, but if Lucifer somehow found out he was attracted to Joan, it would give the fallen angel more leverage.

"I don't know. I mean, this isn't the happiest area anyway, and in the last week or two, it's got quite depressing. I really hate coming here now, but I can't leave the girls without condoms and the homeless without supplies. It's not right." Joan rubbed her hands up and down her arms.

Christian rolled his eyes. "I'm sure they wouldn't miss what they don't have. Living on the streets teaches you to do with very little. You could be spoiling them by giving them all those things."

"What the hell do you know about living on the streets? You're worth millions of dollars, and I bet you've never slept in anything less than a five star hotel." She motioned toward the alley. "It's bad enough to be out in the weather during the summer. During the winter, it's so cold that people can die from it."

He bit his tongue to keep from telling her that he had spent many years without shelter, dealing with the freezing cold before the world had gotten civilized. She wouldn't believe him, and he couldn't blame her, or anyone else.

The belief in angels might be easy for mortals, but to actually see a fallen one in front of them made it difficult. Most would think he was crazy.

"I have dealt with the homeless before, and not just by donating to shelters and foundations to help them." Christian turned to move toward the warehouse. "I don't live in an ivory tower, no matter what others think."

Her muffled laugh drew his attention, and he glanced back at her. "What's so funny?"

"One of my friends said he was shocked you came down from your ivory tower to see how the ordinary people live." She shook her head. "It just struck me funny that you both said the same thing."

"Your friend has been reading too many gossip rags," he muttered, annoyed that someone who didn't know him was talking about him like he was completely out of touch with mortals around him.

"Maybe, but he said he'd done some business with you, and trust me, Lucian is much like you, so it's a lot like the pot calling the kettle black."

Footsteps coming up behind him warned him that Joan had followed as he headed for the building. He paused, waiting for her to catch up. When she came up beside him, he glanced at her.

"What are you doing?"

"I'm not staying out here by myself. You're right. There's no one around except for us, and knowing that makes my creeped out feeling even worse." She shuddered.

"Then go home. It's not safe to be wandering around abandoned buildings late at night without any light and no way of knowing whether there are junkies hiding in the shadows." He pushed open one of the barely hanging doors, wincing at the screeching sound the hinges made.

"How are you going to protect yourself if someone attacks you? Two are better than one, don't you think?" She fisted her hand in his shirt, and Christian inhaled at her touch.

He hesitated just inside like he was letting his eyes adjust to the darkness, even though he didn't need to do that. His power was such that even if he couldn't see with his eyes, he was able to sense if there were others in the warehouse with them.

The place seemed to be deserted, so he figured it wouldn't be too dangerous for Joan to accompany him. Christian wasn't willing to admit he wanted to keep her close simply because he loved the way she smelled. Rolling his eyes, he gave himself a mental slap. *Keep your mind on the job. Don't get distracted.*

"I don't remember doing business with a Lucian," he said as he fidgeted with his pocket like he was pulling something out. Using a small amount of power, he caused a flashlight to pop into existence. He should've thought to bring one along, but he hadn't decided to come and look at the warehouse until after he'd talked to Samantha.

He flicked it on, and Joan gasped at the sudden appearance of light. Swinging the beam around the room, he wrinkled his nose at the sight of all the garbage strewn across the cement floor. *God, mortals can be such pigs at times.*

Joan sighed. "It breaks my heart to see places like this."

"Why? The people who stay here have the choice of keeping it clean and neat. They can find someplace to throw their trash and don't need to piss in the corners of the place where they sleep." Christian gritted his teeth.

"That's not fair. Some of them are mentally ill, and shouldn't be on the street at all. They're the ones who are thrown away by society instead of being helped."

There was a tone in Joan's voice that intrigued Christian. He studied her for a second. "Were you homeless at one point in your life? Is that why you feel so protective of these people?"

She stiffened and he wondered if she thought he was sneering at her. He played back what he'd said and how he'd said it. Cringing inside, he realized he might have come across as being snobby.

"I'm sorry if I sounded as if I was making fun of you or looking down my nose at you. I know what it's like to be without a home. To know that no matter what you do, you're never going to be able to go back to the one place you love the most."

Chapter Four

Sadness colored Christian's words so much that Joan could feel tears well in her eyes. She wasn't sure she believed he could ever understand what being homeless had been like for her. From what she'd seen, he'd always been rich and living above the dirty streets, but the tone of his voice told her Christian did feel something.

"What do you miss? How do you know what it's like to miss something so bad that you'd make a deal with the devil to get it back?"

She took a step back when Christian swung around before grabbing her arm.

"You didn't make a deal with him, did you?"

"Who? The devil?" Joan chuckled. "He doesn't exist, along with angels and God. They're just concepts that help the rest of us deal with things we can't explain."

Christian looked surprised at her words. "You struck me as a person who believed in a higher power. Someone who watched over you."

"Sure. I do have someone to watch over me. For some strange reason, Lucian, my friend, has declared himself my guardian and protector. He's helped me out a lot from the moment I decided to stop drinking and get my life back on track."

"So you were joking about making a deal with the devil?" Christian seemed completely serious when he asked the question.

She smiled. "It's an expression. Of course I was joking, Christian. The devil doesn't exist. No matter how much we would like to blame all the bad things that happen in the world on a fictional being who leads us astray, there's no one to blame but ourselves."

Christian exhaled as he let her go. "I wish that were true," he murmured while turning back to walk across the empty warehouse.

Joan had learned to fear the dark after living on the streets for three years while fighting her alcoholism. She didn't think demons lurked in the shadows, but dangerous people did. Just the thought of being left on her own in the abandoned building had her dashing over the floor to where Christian stood in the middle of the cavernous room.

"What are you doing?"

He held up his hand, wanting her either to stop walking or talking. She did both since she did want to know, and it would be much easier to do as he said and keep him happy. Joan could wait all night from him to speak as long as she was standing next to him.

Finally, he shuddered as if shaking off a blanket, then swung the flashlight around to shine it in her face. "Why are you still here?"

As much as she didn't want him to think she was a wimp, she didn't see the point in lying to him. "I'm scared of the dark, so I wasn't about to walk back to where I can flag down a cab."

He huffed in annoyance. "Fine. I'll escort you to a better area, then will you leave?"

"I'm not leaving you here alone. Just because no one is here right now doesn't mean they won't show up later. They'd jump you for the flashlight alone."

"We've already had this conversation. I can take care of myself when I need to." After shooting a quick look around the room, he gestured for her to go back to the door they'd come in through. "Let's get you to your apartment. You shouldn't be out here by yourself any way. Where are your friends?"

Joan let him take her arm and lead her from the warehouse. She tried to ignore how her nipples hardened and her thighs clenched at the warmth of his fingers on her skin. She took a deep breath, filling her lungs with the scent of his—probably very expensive—cologne.

Imagining what it would feel like to have Christian trail those long fingers of his over her body, she wasn't looking where she was walking and tripped over the threshold of the door. Christian caught her in his arms, crushing her tight against his chest.

Holy shit! He was hiding some nice muscles under his designer T-shirt and a good sized bulge under the zipper of his faded jeans. She tried to swallow her moan, but from the way Christian tensed under her hands, she was pretty sure she hadn't managed it.

"Are you okay?" His hot breath washed over her ear when he asked.

She shivered, need racing down her spine to gather in her pussy, making her wet with desire. "I'm fine."

Her voice came out breathy, and Christian's chest expanded as he inhaled, like he could smell her lust.

"Hmm..." His hum sounded disbelieving.

Christian placed a knuckle under her chin to lift it. Joan lost all thought of protesting the minute his lips touched hers. She slid her hands up his arms to wrap around his shoulders, letting him pull her even closer.

She gasped, allowing him to slip his tongue into her mouth, and she gave over control of the kiss. He tilted her head in a different angle so he could take it deeper. All Joan could think was how she wanted his mouth on other parts of her body. He trailed kisses over her jaw and down her neck then pressed a kiss on the fluttering pulse at the base of her throat like he knew what she was thinking.

"Oh," she whispered as he reached under her shirt to cup her breast in his hand. "Please."

Christian eased an inch or two away, then said, "Please what? I want to hear you tell me exactly what you want."

"I want your mouth on my breasts."

He grunted, seemingly surprised that she hadn't shied away from saying what she wanted. She'd been with enough men to know that hinting didn't always work. Most of the guys she'd slept with were only interested in getting their rocks off. They weren't interested in making sure she came.

"I think that could be arranged, but maybe we shouldn't do anything more here. Might get picked up by the police for public exposure or something." He squeezed her breast hard before stepping back. "We need to get out of here."

Joan took a couple of calming breaths, then nodded. "We'll grab a cab, and go to my place."

"No. We'll go to mine."

Joan usually didn't go with strange men to their apartments. Serial killers didn't always look crazy, so she avoided taking risks like going with them. Yet she'd just gone into an abandoned warehouse with Christian, which probably hadn't been a good idea either.

Christian cradled her cheek in his hand. "I promise I'm not a killer, and I'm not going to keep you tied up in my guest bedroom either."

How did he know what she'd been thinking? Of course, her expression had most likely given her thoughts away.

"It's a little too late for me to be worry about being alone with you now, isn't it?" Joan placed her hand over the zipper of Christian's jeans then rubbed. "I'll take my chances at your place."

"You're not shy, are you?" Christian rocked his hips, pushing his fabric-covered erection against her palm.

She laughed. "No point in it. I want you and you want me. Why should we play games when we could be in your bed doing other things?"

Christian leaned over to place a hard kiss on her lips then he straightened. "Let's go."

Joan didn't say anything else, just followed him toward the street where they could find a taxi. They stepped onto the sidewalk, and a cab almost immediately pulled over. No surprise that they didn't have to wait. In fact, she wouldn't have been shocked if Christian had his own car and driver, though it didn't look like he'd driven there himself.

After climbing in, Christian gave the cabbie his address then settled back against the seat. She smiled at him as he placed his hand on her thigh before inching it up to rub his pinkie over the seam of her jeans.

Biting her lip, she kept from making a sound as he continued to tease her with his touch. It was all she could do not to ask him to unbutton her jeans and slide his hand inside her panties.

"Don't worry," he murmured, leaning close to her. "We're almost to my place."

Again, it was like he was reading her mind, but she was glad to hear him say that. Joan pulled her phone out of her back pocket as she remembered she was supposed to let Cecila know that she was all right.

Done for the night.

She sent the text and jumped when Christian nibbled on her earlobe. A minute later, her phone buzzed.

Good. Heading home to bed?

"Are you going to tell her that you're going to a bed, but it's not yours?" Christian tongued the sensitive spot right behind her ear this time.

Going to Christian Vosberg's apartment with him. I'll text you in the morning, so you know he hasn't chopped me up in a million pieces.

Christian shot her a questioning glance when she showed him the message she'd sent. "Isn't she going to freak out since we've only met once before?"

Joan shook her head. "No. Cecila trusts my judgment for the most part. She'll worry, but she's not going to come hunting us unless I don't text her in the morning."

"I'll have to make sure to remind you to do that. I'd hate to have your friends dislike me, or think I killed you in your sleep." He nuzzled her temple. "I'm not that far gone yet."

Those last words were whispered softly, and Joan had the feeling she wasn't meant to hear them. Deciding to let that statement go for the moment, she made up her mind to enjoy the evening and not worry about the rest of the world.

The driver pulled up to the curb and Christian paid him before they climbed out. He rested his hand at the small of her back, encouraging her to head inside.

The building wasn't one of the modern steel and glass constructs that could be found throughout the city, rather this building's façade was brick, and the lobby floor was marble. She marveled at the old world charm of the place, like stepping back into the nineteen-twenties. If a woman dressed as a flapper walked past her, Joan wouldn't have been shocked.

"This is a wonderful old building. How long have you lived here?" she asked as they stepped onto the elevator.

"Since I came to live in New York." Christian took a card out of his back pocket then slipped it into a slot above the floor buttons in the panel.

"I expect you'd never want to leave." She leaned against the mirrored wall.

"Why would I? I own the entire building. My apartment takes up the top floor, and I don't have to pay rent. There's no reason for me to ever leave." Christian shrugged. "Though I do go away on business quite frequently."

"Where are you from originally, Christian?" Joan hadn't done any other searching on the internet after Piet had told her who Christian was, and now she was glad. She wanted to learn about him in his own words.

Christian's frown held a hint of sadness, and she wondered if his hometown was what he'd been talking about when he'd said he understood what it was like to be homeless.

"A small little town, barely a dot on a road map. You wouldn't have heard of it. Came to the city when I was fifteen to try to make a living."

Joan laid her hand on his arm. "You fulfilled that dream."

He covered her hand with his. "I didn't have anything else to focus on. Did all the jobs I could find to have enough money to put a roof over my head, then I caught a break and started making good money."

The bell dinged and the doors opened right into Christian's foyer. Joan gasped as she left the elevator. Gleaming hardwood floors greeted her gaze, along with brightly painted walls. Christian walked farther into the apartment, and Joan couldn't do anything except follow.

The living room boasted a black leather couch and recliner. A large screen TV hung on the wall in front of the furniture. There was a stone fireplace and a bank of ceiling to floor windows, showcasing the beautiful New York skyline. She ran her hand over the supple leather, enjoying how soft it felt.

Everywhere she looked, there was artwork and furniture that spoke of money and class. It sure beat her little studio apartment, yet she wasn't ashamed of her place. It was what she could afford on her own. She didn't count on anyone else helping her with her bills. Standing on her own two feet was important to her.

"Come here."

Christian wrapped one of his arms around her waist, dragging her close to him before kissing her. She buried her fingers in his hair as she opened for him. His embrace seemed demanding in a way that she'd never experienced before. There was also something desperate in it, like he was searching for an emotion or feeling, and hoped she would provide it for him.

Finally when her lungs burned because of lack of oxygen, she broke the kiss. Christian just went to nibbling and sucking on her neck. With his free hand, he started unbuttoning her shirt. Stopping him never crossed her mind.

It didn't hurt that he was a walking Greek god, and she wasn't going to run away from the attraction. Oh no. She was going to savor it like the most expensive champagne she'd ever tasted. Sex and lust were the closest things she could find that would bring her the same buzz that liquor had.

Cool air drifted over her heated flesh when Christian finished opening her shirt, then pushed the edges aside to bare her chest. Before Joan could think about that, he'd stripped off her shirt and her bra.

"So beautiful," Christian whispered before he bent to take one of her nipples in his mouth.

Joan arched her back, loving the wet warmth as he sucked on her flesh. She jumped, startled when he pinched her other nipple hard, seeming not to want it feeling left out. He tugged then licked, and Joan rocked her hips into his.

Christian continued to worship her breasts, and no matter how hard she tried to get him to stand up so she could undress him, he was having none of it.

She'd never thought her breasts were so sensitive, but she was afraid if he kept it up, she'd come in her jeans, and she really wanted him to be fucking her when she orgasmed for the first time that night.

"Christian, please. I want to be naked with you in your bed," she pleaded as she gripped his hair tight and pulled a little.

Grunting, he looked up at her then slowly inched away, even though he seemed reluctant to let go of her. She waved vaguely in the direction of the rest of the apartment.

"I want to see your bedroom, and then I want you to fuck me on your bed. I want you buried so deep inside me, we get lost in each other."

"All right. Lead the way." He motioned for her to go on.

It took a moment for her to get her legs moving, but once she was sure she could take a step without falling over, Joan straightened. Yet she didn't move, simply looked at him.

"What are you waiting for?" he asked.

"This isn't my place. I don't know where your bedroom is," she pointed out and smiled.

Christian chuckled. "Right. Apparently all the blood has left my brain and pooled in my dick. You made me forget where I was."

She took that as a compliment, laughing as he grabbed her hand to drag her down the hallway toward the back of the penthouse. Again she felt a surge of pride, knowing that she'd turned calm and collected Christian into kind of a bumbling fool.

Shocked they'd made it to the bedroom without breaking something, Joan didn't say a word as Christian began to strip in front of her. She worked on her own clothes while she watched him.

Smooth, tanned skin was revealed with each inch he lifted the shirt, making her fingers itch to touch. When he pulled his T-shirt off and tossed it into a corner, Joan didn't stop herself. Trailing her fingers over firm pectoral muscles, she absorbed the warmth radiating from his skin.

Joan flicked one of his flat, copper-colored nipples, and he inhaled sharply. "Sensitive, are we?"

"I've never been before," he said, looking rather intrigued by how his body reacted to Joan.

"Hmm…must just be our intense physical attraction, huh?" Joan winked at him before she leaned forward to lap at the hardened bud.

Christian jerked, but didn't move away. In fact, he ran his hands over her shoulders, then down to her hips. He kept his hold loose, not stopping her from doing whatever she wanted. And what she wanted was to get a look at his cock.

He balanced her as she sank to her knees then fumbled with the buttons of his jeans to get them undone. Once they were, she pushed both the jeans and his underwear down, freeing his cock to her gaze.

She hummed her pleasure at the sight of his erection. It was thicker than some of the others she'd had over the years, but not as long. Yet she knew it would feel perfect inside her when they got to that part of the night. Leaning in, she rubbed her cheek along his length, loving the way it felt like velvet over an iron rod.

A shudder shook Christian as Joan took him into her mouth, and he moaned. She swirled her tongue around the flared head of his cock then pressed the tip of it into his slit.

"Fuck," he swore, threading his fingers through the locks of her hair to hold her, or maybe he wanted to hold her so he could stand up.

Joan didn't care and the slight tug of his hands on her head kept her from getting too caught up in the blowjob. She needed him to fuck her, so she wouldn't get him off yet, but she did want to taste him. As she started to bob her head, he began to thrust, and they found a rhythm that they both enjoyed.

She must have ended up losing track of time because she came back to herself when Christian tapped her cheek. Looking up into his dark blue eyes, she saw desire and lust burning in them.

"I think we need to get naked and to the bed or I'm going to come in your mouth," he told her.

After letting him slide out, she nodded. "Good idea."

He helped her to her feet without any more talking. Before she climbed onto the mattress, Christian caught her then brought her into his arms. Her heart stopped beating for a second when their naked bodies touched from chests to knees.

He shared his breath with her when they kissed, and Joan wondered why it felt like the most important moment of her life, even more important than kicking her drinking problem and finally getting off the streets. Could it be that all of her days of living on this earth had been leading up to this second as Christian wrapped his arms around her, surrounding her with his heat and scent?

The kiss went on longer than Joan ever thought it would. Neither of them was in a hurry any more to get down to the sex part. There seemed to be something far more intimate about sharing kisses and air until it became too much, and she broke it off. Chest heaving, she stared up at Christian, and his rather wild-eyed stare told her he was as freaked out by the whole encounter as she was.

"I want you," she admitted, "probably more than I've ever wanted another man. What are you? Some kind of incubus or something?"

He answered, "Incubi are just true demons trying to find ways of suck souls from mortals."

"What?" Confused, Joan studied him. "True demons? You do realize that demons aren't any more real than angels, the devil or God."

She could only describe the look he gave her as pitying, but he didn't try to correct her. All he did was pick her up and toss her onto the bed. She shrieked as she bounced.

Christian dug in the nightstand next to the bed for second before joining her. Joan spread her legs, letting him settle between them. Sighing, she allowed her head to drop back on the pillow as he nuzzled the curve of her breast. She traced the bumps in his spine then eased her fingers over his shoulder blades.

Two thin, ragged scars on his back teased her, and she wondered what they were about. How did he get two identical wounds like that? It was almost as if they'd been inflicted on purpose.

He tensed as she touched them then when she moved away from them, he relaxed. So whatever they were from was a touchy subject and not one she should talk about at the moment. Joan gave a mental shrug, doubting they were going to be best friends after this night.

That's all it is. Just one night together, and I'll never see him again. Christian doesn't strike me as the type of guy who slums very often.

So she'd enjoy the experience and look back on it fondly after they parted ways in the morning. Christian took her nipple between his teeth before tugging gently, getting her attention.

"Oh, my God," she groaned, arching her hips off the bed in a need to get closer to him. Her pussy was wet from want, and she was impatient to have him fuck her. "Please, Christian. I want you in me now."

His chuckle sounded rather hoarse like he didn't find reasons to laugh very often. It made her happy to know that she'd gotten him to smile a few times since she'd run into him at the warehouse.

"As you wish." He rocked back on his heels, then opened a foil packet.

Joan watched him roll the rubber over his cock and licked her lips. He was an impressive man, that was for sure. He positioned himself at her opening and met her gaze as he pressed in.

Holding her breath, Joan relished the way he filled her slowly, but with no sign of stopping. She exhaled when he was seated as deep into her as he could go. Their gazes were locked for the entire process, but just the feel of him in her most private of places caused her to close her eyes for a moment. She needed to adjust to the feeling that she was baring her entire soul to a stranger.

"Are you okay?" His question brimmed with concern and she could feel his tension in the way his arms trembled where they were braced on the bed next to her.

Was she okay? Joan wasn't sure how to answer that—it was another of those moments where the next few minutes would change her life on some molecular level that she didn't even realize.

"We don't have to do this."

Christian's being willing to stop right then and there, even if it meant he'd have blue balls for a while until he could take care of his hard-on, was enough to convince Joan she was being silly. Opening her eyes, she nodded.

"Yeah, I'm fine. You can move any time now." She tightened her inner muscles and Christian grunted.

He slid out then plunged back in. Each thrust was harder and faster than the one before. Joan encircled her legs around his waist as she undulated with him, finding that rhythm they'd discovered while she'd been blowing him.

She cried out when he reached between them to rub his thumb over her clit. Pleasure shot through her like needles of electricity, causing her to shiver with need.

"More, Christian. Please," she pleaded, and thankfully he listened.

The scent of sweat and sex filled the air around them as Christian drove Joan to the heights of lust.

"Holy fuck!" She shouted as her orgasm crashed over her in enormous waves of 'omigod, that was the best sex I've ever had' joy.

As she trembled in her own seconds of wishing it would never end, Christian joined her when his climax hit him. Shuddering, he filled the condom with his seed, and for the first time, Joan wished they had done it without protection. Yet while she *was* on the pill, she wouldn't risk catching anything from her lover, and she didn't know anything about Christian.

She winced when he pulled out, and he touched her thigh.

"Did I hurt you?"

"No. It's just been a few months since I've done this, and you're a little thicker than the last guy." She giggled at the look of pride that flashed across his face at her statement. "You men are so infantile. Happy to know your dick's bigger than some stranger's."

After rolling on to her side, Joan watched Christian make his way to what she assumed was the bathroom to get rid of the condom. The sound of running water soothed her, and she closed her eyes as exhaustion swept over her.

The dip in the mattress informed her that Christian had returned. He settled behind her then rested his arm at her waist, pulling her back against him. She grinned as he brushed a kiss over the nape of her neck.

"What time do you have to get up tomorrow?"

"I have to be at work at eight, so I should be out of here by six," she murmured.

"All right. I'll set the alarm."

Her long day and night without much sleep caught up with her, and she drifted asleep, warm and feeling oddly safe in Christian's embrace.

Chapter Five

Christian pulled his pants on over his hips, but before he could fasten them, the rumpled sheets on his bed caught his attention. Joan had rushed out shortly after the alarm had gone off, blowing him a kiss as she left. He imagined if he buried his face in the pillow she'd used, it would smell like her, and what did it say about him that he was tempted not to change his sheets?

"Idiot," he muttered, then finished dressing.

"I see you decided Joan might have information you'll need for the unrepentants."

He didn't react to Mika'il's appearance in the corner of the room. "I don't think she has any information."

Mika'il followed him from bedroom and down the hall to where the coffeepot was brewing in the kitchen. After taking two mugs out of the cupboard, he set one on the counter by the archangel, then poured himself a cup. He got out milk and sugar, knowing that Mika'il liked his coffee sweet.

Christian sat at the table, sipping while he waited for Mika'il to finish what he was doing, and talk to him.

"If she doesn't have any information, then what were you two doing?" Mika'il asked.

"Seriously?" Christian couldn't believe Mika'il had asked that. "You have to ask what we were doing? I know you don't have sex, but I'm pretty sure you know what goes on when two people go to bed together."

"I've had sex." Mika'il paused, then continued, "You slept with her?"

He shrugged. "That's usually what happens when two people who are attracted to each other end up in bed together."

Mika'il shot to his feet before pacing the floor. "I can't believe you'd do something like that."

Christian snorted. "Why are you shocked that I chose to sleep with her? It's not like I haven't slept with other mortals."

"I know, but not in years. I thought you were losing yourself in the darkness, Christian. That's why I gave you this job, and made Dominic call you to Chicago. You need to get involved in the world around you again. You can't start isolating yourself, or you'll lose the very thing that makes you an angel."

Shooting to his feet, Christian heard his chair hit the floor behind him. "An angel? I'm not an angel any more, Mika'il. Remember you took my wings? You and the Father took the very essence of what I was from me. I lost everything I ever wanted or needed a long time ago, and I'm never going to get that back."

Mika'il paused in the midst of his pacing, and turned to face him. "You're the one who chose to fall. You didn't rebel like the others. I never truly understood what you were thinking when you gave up Heaven for this."

The archangel waved his hand around, and Christian took his gesture to mean Earth, not just his apartment. As much as he wanted to punch Mika'il on general principle and for taking his wings, Christian knew he couldn't do that. It wasn't truly fair to lay all of his pain and anger on his oldest friend. Mika'il was right. He had chosen to leave Heaven and the presence of God for the dirt and decay that was the mortal world. At the time, he'd thought he had a valid reason to do it, but he'd found out that there was no reasoning with God.

"I chose to leave because I wanted to prove that God did love us, and he did care about us. Little did I know that there is no leeway with him, and that once I left, I was done. I was one of Lucifer's fallen, to be abandoned by the Father and all my fellow angels." Christian took his mug over to the sink then dumped out his coffee. After setting the cup down, he rested his hands on the edge of the counter. "I suffered because I believed he'd take us all back. That his forgiveness and love for us was stronger than his anger about Lucifer's rebellion."

"He does love you all, Christian. If he didn't, he wouldn't have given you the option of becoming an Enforcer. Do you understand how important it is that he didn't just throw you all away? He might have had me take your wings, but he didn't have me strip you of your power," Mika'il pointed out. "He has given you a way to redeem yourself."

"How exactly am I supposed to do that? By destroying my fellow angels? They might have turned their backs on him, but they don't deserve to die any more than the mortals that he loves do." Christian threw his hands in the air. "We've been over this a thousand times, Mika'il. You can't convince me that he's done this out of love, and I have to admit I'd rather you didn't try to save me from going insane. Right now, it's looking better than the other choice, which is to stay here and continue to destroy people I thought of as family."

Christian didn't take the time to form a mental image of a place in his mind. He gathered his power and dissolved, wanting to be somewhere other than in Mika'il's presence. When he appeared again, he was standing on the observation deck of the Empire State Building. He waited for a second while his brain adjusted to the sudden change.

"Why are you here? Are you following me?"

He jumped at the sound of Lucifer's voice. Turning slowly, he hoped he wouldn't see the fallen angel anywhere. Hoped that those questions were his imagination, not reality. No such luck.

Lucifer stood as close as he could get to the edge of the platform. Christian had the feeling that Lucifer would prefer to climb right out on the edge to look down on the city, but the barriers kept him from doing so. Of course, he could just use his power to get on the other side if he wanted.

"I wouldn't follow you back into Heaven if we were allowed there again," Christian said as he strolled closer to where Daystar stood.

Lucifer laughed, and Christian remembered when he would've joined in, swept up in the joy that had colored his friend's voice. Yet his laugh now mimicked the peal of a broken church bell, off key and sad.

"I remember the days when you and I would spend all of our time looking out for these mortals. They're so fragile and their lives are so short in the grand scheme of the universe." Lucifer turned to look at

Christian. "Then it all went to hell, and here we are, adversaries. You're still protecting them while atoning for something you didn't even do."

"And what are you doing? Are you atoning for something or are you just trying to hurt them?" He shoved his hands in his pockets as he moved to stand shoulder to shoulder with Lucifer. "It's my job to keep you and your fellow unrepentants from doing any more damage to them then you already do."

"Ah, yes. That's right. I'm the evil devil who convinces the world that I don't exist, so I can take it over, one poor pathetic soul at a time." Lucifer threw his arms wide, then spun around in a circle. "You do understand that I could take over at any point in time. It doesn't matter how many Enforcers there are. My power is greater than even yours, Christian. Such is my right as the one who holds dominion over earth."

Christian pursed his lips as he breathed in deeply. "Yes, I'm perfectly aware of what you are capable of. I guess I've always wondered why you haven't done it. I would've thought that you would have taken advantage of your place to ruin the lives of the mortals you see as weaker than you."

Lucifer shot him a look. "Maybe you should do some more thinking about that. Maybe there are other reasons why I'm here, and doing what I do, instead of searching for my touch in all the bad things that happen around the world."

"I'm looking into the gathering of several unrepentants at abandoned warehouses here in the city. Do you have anything to do with that?"

Sure, Daystar could lie to him about it, but Christian had never thought his friend was a liar. Lucifer was much like Mika'il in the way he would evade most questions he didn't want to answer, so Christian figured he could trust Lucifer.

"Do you think I'm gathering my minions to take over the city?" Lucifer paused, as he seemed to think about that idea before he continued, "I don't have minions, Christian. You know that. I can barely tolerate you when I run into you. I'm certainly not going to be able to endure any of the crazy fallen for any length of time. I'm not their leader anymore. The instant Mika'il took their wings, they turned their backs on me."

"They see you as the one who led them astray. You were the one who said angels should hold a more important place in God's heart than mortals. You were the one who wanted to be like God." Christian couldn't help but remind Lucifer of his rallying cry.

Lucifer grunted. "Did I say all those things?"

"Yes."

"What a pretentious jackass I was," Lucifer murmured.

Christian slapped his former friend on the shoulder. "I've been telling you that since the fall. Now, do you have anything to do with them gathering?"

"Of course I don't. I have no need for them to help me with anything. I'm doing fine on my own." Lucifer glanced down at the Rolex on his wrist. "I must be going. I have to visit a friend."

Before Christian could overcome his amazement that Lucifer had friends, the fallen was gone, and Christian was left wondering who Lucifer would go and visit in the city.

"Sir, I've got some information about Phillip and the unrepentants." Samantha's voice interrupted Christian's musing.

"*Good. I'll meet you at the same coffee shop as before,*" he informed her as he gathered his power once more.

"*Yes, sir.*"

Within a minute or two, Christian was standing in front of the café. He went in and ordered while he waited for Samantha to show up. He had a feeling he knew what she was going to tell him, and he wasn't looking forward to cleaning up the mess.

Christian sat, knowing it would take Samantha a little while to get there. She wasn't as powerful as he was, so travel took a little longer for her. As he waited, he pulled out his phone to check his messages. He smiled when he saw something from Joan.

Hey there. Had a great time last night.

He typed in a return message.

Me too. Are you busy tonight?

Have class after work, but get out at ten.

Pausing for a moment, he thought about his response. Was he really thinking about maybe starting a relationship? How could he be sure Joan was even interested in having more than just sex with him? Maybe she only wanted a fuck buddy because she certainly seemed confident about getting what she wanted.

"*Why not do it? You need to make some connections to other people again. It'll keep you on this side of sane.*"

"*I hate it when you pop into my head like that,*" Christian complained as Mika'il laughed.

"*I know. Why do you think I do it? Go and sleep with her again. Sex is good for you.*"

Christian blinked at the rather incredulous feeling of having the archangel tell him sex was good for him. He decided that maybe no reply was the best answer. Before he could stop himself, he typed again.

Want to get together? I can pick you up after school.

Great. I'll send you the address. See you at ten.

See you then.

He sensed Samantha's presence as she entered the café. After tucking away his phone, he gestured for her to come over. She dodged the other customers, and the frown on her face told Christian she was upset about something.

Flopping in the chair across from him, Samantha heaved a loud sigh. Christian pushed one of the coffees he'd gotten over to her.

"Thank you," she said before taking a sip.

"Welcome." He waited while she drank a little bit before he asked, "What did you find out?"

"Phillip was heading to this warehouse when he disappeared." She held out a piece of paper. "From what I've dug up, he wasn't expecting any unrepentants to be there. Everything he found out said they had moved on to a different place."

"Yet they were there."

She nodded, and Christian resisted the urge to rub his neck. It sounded like not only were they gathering, they were organized enough to plot the death of an Enforcer. He had no doubt that they had left clues for Phillip to follow because they'd wanted to get him alone. Only Christian was strong enough to deal with several fallen at a time, but he had the feeling he might need to call in some help.

"Does anyone have any idea how many of them we're dealing with?" He pulled out his phone, then glanced at Samantha.

"Between ten and fifteen. At least that's what I've been able to put together while looking around. Phillip didn't have a chance." Her hands shook before she wrapped them around her cup.

"So it appears," Christian muttered as he scrolled through numbers on his phone. When he got to the right one, he punched the send button. While it rang, he tapped his fingers on the table.

"Celeste Montgomery," a female answered.

"This is Christian Vosberg. We met in Chicago." He leaned back in his chair, staring at the crowd mingling behind Samantha, yet not seeing any of them.

Celeste hummed softly. "Right. I remember, Christian. What can I do for you?"

"I have ten to fifteen unrepentants who seem to be joining forces here in the city. I'm not sure why."

"Has Lucifer been sighted anywhere in the city? He could be gathering the other fallen for some kind of coup," Celeste suggested.

Christian shook his head, even though she couldn't see him. "I talked to Lucifer earlier this morning. He says he has nothing to do with this."

Two unladylike sounds rang in his ears.

"You believed him?" Celeste sounded perplexed that Christian could consider Lucifer was telling the truth.

"Yes."

"How can you believe that creature? He was the one who lead us all astray. Lucifer told us that we should be equal to God because of our powers. He lied, yet

74

you think he wouldn't lie about this?" Celeste shouted.

He held the phone away from his ear as she continued her diatribe about Lucifer for a few more minutes before he said, "Enough."

Samantha blinked at the command in his voice and Celeste fell silent.

"You fell because of your own hubris. You and your fellow fallen wanted to believe in what Lucifer was selling. Don't lay all of the blame on his shoulders. You must take some of it because you chose to listen." Christian looked at Samantha while he told Celeste off, hoping she got what he was saying as well.

"Fine. So you do believe him when he told you he has nothing to do with these unrepentants?" Celeste now sounded annoyed.

"Yes, because he has nothing to gain by lying to me. The one thing I can always trust is that Lucifer will tell me the truth. Most of the time, he knows it pisses me off, so he does it to get a reaction from me." Christian clenched his hand. "I need you and Bradford to come to New York to help me deal with this group. You won't have to do anything with Lucifer. I can pretty much guarantee he won't make an appearance while you are around."

Celeste coughed, seeming taken aback by Christian's request. "You need help?"

As much as it irked him to have to ask, he said, "Would you and Bradford be so kind as to join me in New York so that we might rid the world of some insane fallens? They've already killed one of my Enforcers."

"I'll call William and get him on the next flight out of Reno. I can be there by tomorrow afternoon, and he will be there in the evening." Celeste didn't seem to be gloating or happy that she'd gotten him to admit he needed help and ask her nicely to come. "I'll call you in the morning with our flight numbers."

"Thank you, and there will be a car and driver waiting to pick you up. He'll bring you to my place." Christian hung up without saying goodbye.

Samantha studied him. "Why are you calling in outside Enforcers to clear out this gang? There are more than enough of us here to do the job."

"Celeste Montgomery is one of the most powerful Enforcers in the country, second only to me. William Bradford is not only an Enforcer, but an Avenger. He'll be able to punish any of the unrepentants who need it." Christian pursed his lips for a second before he said, "In my opinion, any of them who helped kill Phillip deserve to be punished."

She didn't look happy, but she wasn't going to argue with him. That was what happened when he was the head Enforcer for the entire East Coast—he got to make the decisions.

"Thank you for getting this address for me, Samantha. I promise you that Phillip will be avenged, and those who killed him taken care of before they do any more harm."

"All right." Samantha finished her coffee, then stood. "If you need anything else, you know how to get a hold of me."

He nodded then watched her walk away. After he stood, he tossed his cup in the trash before he left as well. He had some recon to do before Celeste and William showed up.

* * * *

Joan walked out of the library, tired but happy. She had finished her term paper and was ready to turn it in in the morning. Only one more class and she'd have her Masters in Social Work. Then she'd be able to do something about the people on the street.

A horn honking drew her attention, and she looked to see that recognizable Jaguar parked at the curb. Christian climbed out before walking around the front of the car to approach her.

Before she could say anything, he encircled her waist then brought her tight to him. She lifted her chin to offer herself to him as he kissed her. Joan gasped, which gave Christian an opening to slide his tongue into her mouth.

She gripped his shoulders as lust swamped her, and her knees went weak. *Holy cow! He can kiss* swept through her mind before it went blank. He cupped her ass in both hands then lifted her up to rub against her mound.

"Get a room," someone muttered as they pushed past him.

Christian eased away, but didn't take his hands off her body. "I was going to be polite and take you out to dinner. Maybe go dancing, but I find that all I want to do is go back to my place and fuck you into the mattress."

"Fine with me," she agreed. Being able to have him moving over her again would be the perfect ending for the night.

Motioning to his car, he said, "Your chariot awaits, my lady."

Joan giggled as she walked over there. "You sound so formal at times, like you grew up in a different era."

"I've been around for quite some time. Far longer than you could ever imagine," he muttered as he opened the door for her.

What exactly did he mean by that? How could any guy sound so weary when Christian could only be around forty years old? Yet his tone of voice sounded more like he was a hundred. After sitting, she put on her seat belt while Christian went around to the driver's side.

She closed her eyes, trusting Christian to get them back to his apartment without any trouble. While Joan rode, she thought about the conversation she'd had with Lucian earlier in the day at the diner.

"You're looking rather chipper this afternoon," Lucian said as he sat in his regular booth. "You must have got some last night, right?"

She set the cup of coffee in front of him and smiled. "As a matter of fact, I did. Do you want the details?"

He shuddered, drawing a chuckle from her. "Have I ever wanted to hear your sexual exploits?"

"No, but it's so much fun to tease you." Joan leaned over to brush a kiss over his cheek. "Thank you for caring about me."

Lucian ducked his head, but not before Joan swore she saw his cheeks turn pink. It tickled her to know she could embarrass a sophisticated man like Lucian.

When she returned with his food, he asked, "Are you going to tell me who the lucky man was?"

"Surprisingly, it was Christian Vosberg. We ran into each other down at one of the abandoned warehouses I go to when I want to talk to some of the working girls. One thing led to another, and I wound up at his apartment." Joan shrugged. "I never thought a guy like him would slum with a girl like me, but you know what? He doesn't seem all that snobby to me."

"It's hard for any guy to seem snobby when he has his dick buried in you," Lucian muttered.

Confused, she stared at him. "Are you jealous?"

"Not jealous. Just pissed off. I was hoping this wouldn't happen because now I have to do something I don't want to do, and I hate being forced into this position." Lucian glared at the table in front of him. "Why couldn't you two have kept your hands off each other?"

"What does me sleeping with Christian Vosberg have to do with you?" Joan was confounded by Lucian's apparent anger at the situation.

Lucian shot to his feet, and the sound of the plate shattering on the floor caused the noise in the diner to stop. Joan met Lucian's dark gaze, and she almost sobbed at the agony she saw there. Whatever Lucian was feeling was hurting him so deeply, Joan almost questioned how the man was still standing.

"It has everything to do with me. You might say that sounds arrogant, but still I'm the one who is stuck in the middle, having to do this horrible thing without being able to have a choice in the matter. I wouldn't wish harm on either one of you, yet harm is what must happen." Lucian cradled Joan's face in his hands. "You're a wonderful girl, Joan. I hope he thinks you're worth what he has to give up."

After saying those cryptic words, Lucian tossed some money on the table before stalking out of the diner. Joan knew she looked like an idiot, with her mouth hanging open and shock on her face. What had set Lucian off? And what kind of history did Lucian and Christian have with each other?

"How do you know Lucian?" she asked without opening her eyes.

Christian grunted. "I told you I don't know any Lucian."

"Well, you might not remember him, but he certainly remembers you. Nearly exploded when he found out we were having sex. I've never seen him this upset, and we've been through a lot of shit together." She twisted in the seat, then looked at Christian.

"What's his last name? I've done business with a lot of people over the years. It's hard to remember most of them."

The way he said that told her it took more energy than he was willing to expand to remember people. Joan thought for a moment, then laughed.

"You know what? I have no idea what his last name is. I don't remember him ever saying it, and for most of our acquaintance, I've been more pre-occupied getting back on my feet than wondering what his name was."

"What does he look like?"

At least Christian was making an effort to talk to her. Joan got the feeling he didn't chat up many people. Of course, she also got the feeling that he was more isolated than she'd thought, considering he could surround himself with an entourage if he'd wanted.

"Lucian could pass for your twin, except he has this weird cross-shaped brand on his left cheek. Also, he has these really strange eyes. No whites, just all black. He said he had a medical condition that caused it."

If she hadn't been looking right at Christian, she never would've noticed him stiffen when she described Lucian. *So he does know him. Interesting.* And by the way they each reacted, what they knew about each other wasn't good.

"Doesn't sound familiar to me, and I guess I would remember a man looking like that if I ever saw him."

"Right." Okay, he was lying, but she didn't call him on it. It really wasn't any of her business at the moment why they chose to dislike one another. "What exactly do you do, Christian?"

"I'm in the protection business, sort of a personal security company." He pulled up to an underground garage, then slid a card through a slot. The gate swung open before he drove through.

"You must be good at it since you have money." She gestured toward the dashboard of the car. "I haven't seen many of these out on the streets."

Christian's smile was full of memories and he shrugged. "I've had a lot of practice keeping people safe. Makes it easy to earn money if you're the best at what you do."

"True."

Chapter Six

He parked in a spot then came around to help her out. She slid her arm through his as they made their way to the elevator. Suddenly, a man stepped from the shadows, and Joan gasped. The stranger's silver eyes traced over her in one quick glance, yet she swore he saw all of her deepest secrets, and in some way found her wanting.

"What do you want, Mika'il?" Christian moved her behind him as he confronted the other man.

"Have you made plans to take care of our little problem?" Mika'il crossed his arms over his chest, unhappiness evident in every inch of his body.

"Yes. Montgomery and Bradford are coming in tomorrow to help me. We'll execute our plan tomorrow night. You're not needed around here."

Mika'il's head reared back like the man had an issue with Christian talking to him like that. "You have another problem as well. She is marked." Mika'il waved toward Joan.

"I know." Christian gripped Joan's hand tightly.

"When did you find out?"

Mika'il's narrow-eyed stare caused Joan to shiver.

"Tonight. I'll deal with it after the other situation is taken care of." Christian started moving in the direction of the elevators again. "You can go away, Mika'il. We will ask for your help if we need it."

Christian's tone said he wasn't planning on asking. Joan just stayed quiet. There were other things at work here besides two men having a pissing contest about a job. There were undertones in their words that reminded her of how Lucian talked sometimes, like there was an entire conversation going on beneath the words he spoke.

Mika'il pointed at Joan. "You must take care of her, Christian. If he finds out that you are with her, he will do everything he can to hurt you."

"I know that. You don't have to remind me how he lives to make my life miserable," Christian said, then snarled. "Just leave, Mika'il. If I need you, I'll call."

Joan blinked, and Mika'il was gone. She hadn't seen him move, and she couldn't hear any footsteps echoing through the concrete garage. Christian took a deep breath, and she rested her hand on his back.

"Have I caused problems for you?" She had received that message loud and clear from Mika'il, even though she didn't know what he meant by her being marked.

"With Mika'il?" Christian punched the call button, then shook his head. "No. I'm often in trouble with him, so what's one more mark on my card? You have created other problems for me."

"Maybe I should just grab a cab and go home," she suggested, not wanting to cause him any trouble. She hadn't spent much time with Christian, but there was something about him that touched her and she didn't want to give him up yet.

The doors opened and Christian tugged her inside the lift. He slid his card for the penthouse then embraced her, making sure they touched from chest to thigh. It was as if he needed her warmth as much as she needed his.

"No. You'll stay with me. I can protect you, and you are causing me no more problems than I encounter most days in my job." Christian nuzzled along her jaw. "I don't know why, but I'm willing to fight for you, Joan. I haven't felt this way in years, and I don't want to lose it, not if it means giving you up."

She encircled his neck before tilting her head to give him access to her neck. "I've never felt this way before either. It's like I've been waiting for you forever, and somehow we were meant to be together, even though I know nothing about you."

He tensed. "I'm not sure you'd believe me if I told about myself."

"Why don't we go to your place, get undressed and climb into bed? We can tell each other all our secrets then." She grinned. "I was going to suggest having drinks as well, but I haven't had one in five years, and I probably shouldn't start again."

"Good idea." Christian led the way into his apartment.

They undressed in silence before slipping under the covers. He brought her close to him until she rested her head on his chest. She trailed her hand over his stomach, entertained by the rippling muscles under his skin.

"I've been wondering how you got those scars on your shoulder blades," she said to break the quiet.

Christian sighed. "I'm not sure how to explain. You don't believe in God, his angels or the devil."

"What do those have to do with the marks?" She wasn't sure where he was going with that line of conversation.

"I'm an angel, or I was an angel until I fell. The marks on my shoulders are from when Mika'il removed my wings." He stopped, and there didn't seem to be anything else to say.

Joan pushed away from him to sit up. She let the sheets pool around her waist as she stared at Christian.

"Mika'il? As in the guy who accosted you in the garage several minutes ago?"

He nodded, but kept quiet.

"You're a fallen angel?" At his second nod, she laughed. "Aren't fallen angels demons? I thought you were all supposed to be crazy and evil."

Christian shifted until he leaned back against the headboard. "Some of us are, and those are the ones I'm charged with dealing with, so they don't hurt mortals."

"Mortals?"

It was sad that Christian was this crazy, because he was certainly the most gorgeous man she'd ever met. *If he's crazy, why aren't you running out of his apartment screaming for the cops?* It was a good question, and Joan wasn't sure she could answer it.

"Yes. Mortals, or humans as you call yourselves. You are God's beloved children, and I'm charged with protecting you from the evils of the unrepentants. I'm an Enforcer, a fallen angel who has agreed to hunt his own kind in order to someday win back his chance at Heaven." Sadness shone in Christian's eyes.

As strange as the conversation was, Joan sensed a current of truth running through his words. She'd never really believed in God, Heaven and all that stuff. She'd pulled herself up from the gutter on her own without help from any angel, unless Lucian counted as one.

"Who is Mika'il?"

Christian grimaced. "He's the Warrior angel, one of God's archangels. He's in charge of the Enforcers, though I'm sure he'd rather allow us to go our own way. Mika'il has a lot of responsibilities, and he doesn't really need to deal with us."

"Why did you fall? Didn't it have to do with Lucifer and his believing in the superiority of angels?" Joan tried to remember what she'd learnt in Sunday school.

"Yes, that was the fall, and it was all Lucifer's fault, though all the angels who participated are to blame for their own actions." Christian fidgeted with the edge of the sheet. "I didn't rebel. I chose to leave Heaven because I wanted to prove that God was forgiving if you ask for it. Little did I know that He wouldn't distinguish between me and those who truly did rebel. He refused me Heaven, and told Mika'il to take my wings. Then Mika'il offered me the position of Enforcer."

"So you're some kind of angelic police officer? Keeping the crazy fallen from hurting mortals?" Joan asked.

"Yes. It's my only hope to get back to where my true home is. My heart doesn't lie here on this earth. It's like having a piece of my soul ripped out of my body to be denied His presence." He reached out to take her hands in his. "Or it used to be. Somehow you've filled that empty spot in my heart, and I'm not sure why."

Joan shrugged. If a former angel didn't have the answer, then she certainly didn't.

"Do you believe me?" He studied her face.

"I can't say I do believe you a hundred percent, but I have to admit that there's an instinctive push from inside of me to accept what you've told me." She rubbed her thumb over Christian's knuckles. "I guess there are worse things you could be."

"I could be a serial killer or a True Demon, those dark creatures on which your nightmares are based," Christian informed her.

"True. Do you want me to tell you my story, or can you read my mind?"

Christian shook his head in denial. "I could, but I never would without your permission. It's an invasion of privacy, whether you know I'm doing it or not. Please, tell me your story. I wish to hear about you."

She took a deep breath. "To be honest, I had a great childhood. Two parents who loved me and a brother who adored me, when he wasn't annoying the shit out of me. Then I went away to school, and nine-eleven happened. Even though I didn't know anyone who died that day, it changed something inside me. I was going to school here in the city, and somehow I lost my sense of security."

Nodding, he squeezed her hand. "That day affected everyone who lived in New York in ways we still haven't figured out."

"I started drinking, and soon was staying as drunk as I could. It dulled the pain inside of me. I was sober for maybe a month out of seven years after nine-eleven. But at my lowest point, when I was kneeling in an alleyway, throwing up nothing but alcohol, I could feel my body dying in a way I'd never felt before. It hit me that I was killing myself and I didn't want to do that anymore."

She remembered that night clearly. She'd managed to get together enough money for some cheap whiskey, then had slunk into the closest alley to drink it. After she'd finished half the bottle, her body had revolted, and she'd started throwing up. There'd been blood on her lips when she'd finished. Like she'd told Christian, she'd been able to feel her body dying, and it had scared her because she hadn't been ready to die.

Tears had flowed from her eyes as she'd tried to get her liquor-soaked brain to work, then she'd felt a presence beside her. Lucian had stood there, his dark eyes gleaming with the promise of help. He'd held out his hand, and she'd taken it, somehow knowing he could give her the strength to get sober and be free of the craving that chewed chunks out of her very soul.

"I got help, and after I was physically healed, I started working on my mental and emotional state. Once that process began, I found a place to live and got a job. In the beginning, it was so difficult to not take a sip of a beer or order a glass of wine, but I got stronger with each day, and now it's only on a rare occasion that I wish I could drink." Joan scooted closer to Christian. "I help out the homeless, the junkies and the street workers because I know what it's like to be where they are. I never did drugs because alcohol was all I could deal with and afford. I believe everyone can be redeemed with a little help."

Christian cradled her face with his hands before brushing a soft kiss over her lips. "You have a good soul, Joan. I'm sure all those you help see you as their guardian angel, and what you do is far more important than my job."

She didn't want to talk anymore. She would think about what Christian had told her the next day, but at the moment, all she wished was that Christian would make love to her. Joan moved his hands then fell over onto her back, pulling him with her.

The moment he settled over her, she sighed, knowing this was where she needed him. Joan needed him to press her into the mattress. Joan wound her leg around his leg before arching up to rub her mound against his length.

"Wait." He rolled away to dig through the drawer again. His triumphant crow as he held up a foil packet made her laugh.

"Hurry," she pushed, wanting him inside her as soon as possible.

After tearing open the packaging, he rolled the rubber over his length. Christian returned to his place between her legs. Joan held her breath as he sank into her wet pussy, and the slow way he did so as if he was staking a claim to every inch of her.

She wanted to be his in every way, and if that meant accepting his story about being an angel, she would think about it because really, what harm was there in him thinking he was a former angel?

All thought left her head when Christian started moving, thrusting in and pulling out in a slow, steady rhythm guaranteed to drive her crazy in a short time. Joan ran her hands over his straining back, tracing the scars, then down to his ass where she took his firm cheeks in a hard grip.

Their lovemaking had the feeling of a dance where they were the only ones who heard the music, and Joan had never had that happen with any of the men she'd slept with before Christian. She was so caught up in the heat roiling off him along with the scent of his sweat that she never noticed when he started moving faster and faster.

Soon he was driving into her, forcing her breath out of her lungs in loud gasps each time he took her.

"Oh, my God," she cried as her orgasm exploded inside her. Her muscles clenched around his erection, milking it as best she could without a working brain to tell her what to do.

"I love you," he whispered right before his climax hit him. Then as he froze deep inside her while filling the condom, he shouted in the dark room.

Joan blinked in confusion. Had he said he loved her? Wasn't it too soon for that? They'd only met a few days ago, and she wasn't sure she believed in love at first sight. Yet she had no other word to describe how she'd felt about him since the minute they'd met and after, when she hadn't been able to forget about him.

He collapsed to the side, and she grimaced as he slid out of her. She settled on her side to watch him take care of the rubber then he turned to face her. She tried to figure out what he was thinking, but his expression was blank.

Did he realize what he'd said during sex or was it something that had slipped out, but he'd never have said it if he'd been in his right mind?

"I do, you know," he said softly.

"You do love me?" She wasn't going to pretend that wasn't what she was thinking about. "How do you know that? We just met the other day. No one falls in love that quickly."

Christian ran his finger down the slope of her nose. "Maybe most don't, but I've been alive long enough to not question how I feel. It's not like we don't have time to get to know each other, and maybe you can learn to love me as well."

Joan grabbed his hand then placed a kiss in his palm. "I think I'm on my way."

He relaxed, and she realized how nervous he'd been about her reaction to his declaration. She traced his features with her gaze, learning the curve of his cheek and the strength of his jaw, trying to etch them permanently on her heart. He was familiar to her in a way that she couldn't really explain, and it didn't have anything to do with his striking resemblance to Lucian.

It was like she'd always known him, and had been waiting for him to return to her. It was a strange feeling, and she would examine it more in the morning. At the moment, all she wanted was to curl up in his embrace and sleep, knowing he would keep her safe.

Christian wound his arms around her waist before pulling her as close as they could get without being one body. Joan gave herself permission to relax, and her pleasant exhaustion drew her under, and she fell asleep listening to Christian's heartbeat.

* * * *

Later the next day, Joan was getting ready to leave Christian's apartment to go to work. He'd been busy planning something with his business associates, but he hadn't told her what it was. He'd simply given her a card key to his apartment, and told her to come back when she got off work.

"I might not be here, but I'd like you to spend the night again. I like the idea of coming home to you sleeping in my bed." He gently pushed a lock of her hair off her forehead.

"All right. I can do that." She stood on her tiptoes to kiss him. "Be careful doing whatever you've got planned for tonight. I hope you're not doing it on your own."

"No. I have some people coming in from out of town to help me. The good thing is that after tonight, there shouldn't be any more of that particular problem."

"Good. I want you safe, so that I can congratulate you on a job well done with a celebratory blow job." She grinned as he groaned. "I have to go now. I'll see you whenever you get back."

As she headed toward the elevator, it dinged and two people stepped from it. The statuesque blonde and the dark-haired man made quite an impressive couple, and Joan felt uncomfortable in her waitress uniform.

"Bradford. Montgomery. I'm glad you could get here on such short notice." Christian rested his hand at the small of her back, urging her forward.

"When you call, Vosberg, we have to obey," the man said, not looking overjoyed to be there.

The woman shook Christian's hand. "It's a problem we all might be facing at some time in our individual cities. We help you here, you repay the favor later on when it's our turn."

Christian dipped his head in acknowledgment of the deal. "Certainly. I'd like to introduce my girlfriend, Joan Fisher. Joan, this is Celeste Montgomery and William Bradford, two of my Enforcer friends."

Both of them looked shocked when Christian told her that, but Joan smiled and shook their hands.

"Christian told me about being a fallen angel and all that. I'm still working on accepting it." She glanced at her watch. "Shit! I have to get out of here or I'm going to be late."

After blowing Christian a kiss, she nodded at the others then walked onto the elevator to go down to the street.

* * * *

"I can't believe you told her about us," Celeste commented as they strolled away from the warehouse.

Christian grimaced at the rip in his jacket. He'd throw it out when he got home. It wasn't like he didn't have the money to buy a new one. When Celeste's comment registered with him, he glanced over at her.

"Why wouldn't I do that? I love her, and she needs to know the truth before she starts falling in love with me. I don't want her stuck with me and not knowing who I really am." He propped his fists on his hips. "How long will it take Bradford to deal with them?"

"Not very long. He's full up on power and none of them were very strong to begin with. I'm surprised they were able to gather together for this long without fighting amongst themselves."

"I'm not. The unrepentants are stronger than you think, Celeste, and they want to survive as much as we do, so they'll try to find ways to do so." Christian rubbed his neck. "I should head back to the apartment. Do you and Bradford have a place to stay?"

Celeste turned to face the warehouse, but Christian knew she was still very focused on him. "Yes. We have rooms at the Waldorf-Astoria. You do know she's marked, right?"

Sighing, Christian rolled his eyes. He should've known she would bring that up.

"Yes, I know, and I didn't realize she was until last night."

"You've never seen him around her? I would've thought he'd keep an eye on his prize." She kept her voice even and calm, though Christian knew she wasn't happy about what was going on.

"I think he's been keeping an eye on her since he marked her. She has a friend called Lucian, and the way she described him fits Lucifer. Yet Joan says he's been nothing but good to her. He's helped her become a recovering alcoholic, and get her life back on track." Christian closed his eyes for a second. "Does that sound like the Lucifer we know?"

"No, but that doesn't mean anything. He's never been predictable, Christian. You know that." She heaved a sigh of annoyance. "I can't tell you what to do, except keep an eye on her if you love her. I don't know how to help Joan. We can't counteract a mark like that."

"I know," he ground out between gritted teeth, and it was that knowledge of helplessness that got to him. "I'm leaving. I'll see you tomorrow for a late lunch before you fly home?"

Celeste nodded, and he left to go back to Joan. He needed to hold her in his arms to help convince him the world is a good place to live.

Chapter Seven

The next morning, Christian finished sliding pancakes on two plates while Joan poured the orange juice. She pinched his ass when he walked by, and he grunted, sending a lust-filled glare at her. She just laughed.

"Did your business go well last night?" she asked as they sat at the kitchen table to eat.

"Yes. It's been taken care of and the mess has been cleaned up." He took a sip of juice before he said, "I told Celeste and William we would meet them for lunch before they flew home."

Joan was amazed that he would want to be seen out in public with her, which she readily admitted was a silly thought. "All right. I don't have school or work today, so I'm free all day."

"Good. Maybe after breakfast, we could go back to bed and work off the calories we ate." He leered at her.

"I never say no when a handsome man wants to take me to bed." She winked.

The elevator doors opened, and they jumped to their feet to see who could've gotten up to the penthouse without being buzzed in.

"It's time, Joan," Lucian said as he walked into Christian's apartment like he owned it.

"What are you doing here, Lucifer?"

"What are you doing here, Lucian?"

She and Christian spoke at the same time. Joan looked over to where Christian stood, hands clenched and face flushed.

"You *do* know him." For some reason that was more important than why Lucian was there. "Lucian said he knew you, but you never said you knew him."

"I don't know him as Lucian, but I do know Lucifer Daystar. We've been opponents for more centuries than I can count."

"Lucifer? His name is Lucian." Joan glanced at her friend, silently imploring him to deny what Christian said.

"No more lies, Joan. I am Lucifer, the most horrible of all fallen angels. The creature mortals seem to fear even more than God." Lucian paused for a moment before continuing, "I never understood why your kind are so scared of me. I mean, I don't hold absolute power over you."

Lucian reached out to touch her cheek, but Christian sprang in between them. Lucian raised his eyebrow, his only sign of surprise.

"Don't touch her," Christian snarled and Lucian stepped back.

Yet Joan could tell it wasn't fear that made Lucian back off. The sadness that always seemed to lurk in Lucian's eyes flared, and Joan had the feeling that Lucian hated what was going on between him and Christian.

"Joan must pay the price, Christian. You can't stop me from taking what is mine," Lucian — or Lucifer since that was his true name — said.

"She probably didn't even know what she was doing when she made the bargain with you. How can you do this? You know what she means to me."

The pain in Christian's voice brought tears to Joan's eyes. She watched Lucifer inhale deeply then straighten his back, seeming to prepare himself for some horrible duty.

"Why do you think I'm doing this? Because I can."

"Right. You could've done this at any point in the past, but now that we're together, you chose to call your debt in." Christian glared at Lucifer. "I don't believe this is a coincidence."

Joan stepped between them, ignoring Christian's protest. "I want to know what the hell is going on. What kind of debt do I owe you, Lucifer? And why don't I remember it? Does this have anything to do with Mika'il saying I was marked?"

"Mika'il knows about her?" Lucifer asked Christian.

"Yes. We met him the other night," Joan answered. "I don't think he was happy about the whole situation."

"No one is happy about any situation I might be involved in," Lucifer pointed out. "I don't have much time. I need to get this taken care of."

"Get what taken care of? Nothing is going to happen until you explain what the fuck is going on." Joan folded her arms and stared at both men.

"You sold your soul to the devil, Joan, and he's here to collect." Christian encircled her waist before pulling her tight to his side.

She tensed. "What? I think I would've remembered that."

Lucifer paced the living room. "Do you remember the last night you drank? You were throwing up in an alley, and you were bleeding from ulcers in your stomach and throat. I'm sure you felt like you were going to die. I found you there, and as I walked up, you said, 'I'd do anything to stop from doing this again'."

Joan sorted through her memories, going back to that night, then she nodded. "I remember saying that, then you showed up and offered me your hand. Was that when we made the deal?"

"Yes. I asked you if you would accept my help for a debt to be paid at a later date. Usually when anyone makes a deal with me, it's for their soul, which I take and use to add to my power." Lucifer spoke as if reading from a script—saying what people expected him to say. It didn't make sense to Joan.

"Why don't I remember that?" Joan frowned as she tried to remember the entire conversation.

Lucifer shrugged. "Most people seem to forget until I return to collect. Not sure why, though I haven't tried that hard to find out."

"You're going to take my soul, and I'll cease to exist...like I died?"

"Yes, and you won't be going to Heaven because I guess no creature without a soul can go there." Lucifer's laugh sounded bitter and angry. "Which is why I'm banned from there, apparently."

Joan turned to look at Christian, shocked to see tears rolling down his cheeks. She couldn't stop from kissing him, the knowledge that it might be the last time they did chasing through her mind. He held her tight like he would never let her go.

She didn't know how long she was lost in his embrace before Lucifer huffed.

"I can't waste any more time. I have other things to do."

"No! Take my soul instead," Christian offered, moving to stand between Joan and Lucifer.

"Christian, you can't," Joan protested as she gripped his arm.

"I'm not letting him have your soul, Joan. Lucifer will be happy to take mine. It's something he's been after for a long time."

Christian met Lucifer's dark gaze, and he frowned at the look of resignation swimming deep in Lucifer's eyes. The strange sadness Christian had often seen in the other fallen's eyes was there as well.

"Are you sure you wish to give up everything for her?" Lucifer gestured toward Joan. Christian nodded. "Joan's given me something I never thought I'd have again."

"What's that?"

Lucifer might have asked the question, but Christian had the oddest feeling he already knew the answer. Turning to face Joan, Christian smiled as he reached out to cradle her face in his hands.

"She gave me my faith back. She showed me that not all humans were selfish and only out for themselves." He heard Lucifer exhale loudly, and shot him a quick glance. "What's that for?"

"Really? She's not selfish and only out for herself? What about all those years where she drank herself into a stupor every night? When her family worried about her and thought she was dead in a gutter somewhere because she never contacted them?"

Lucifer would've gone on listing all of Joan's past transgressions, but Christian wasn't interested in hearing them. He didn't care what she'd done before he met her, just like she didn't care what he had done all those millions of years ago when he'd fallen.

Of course, his actions could be considered worse than hers, and his consequences were far direr as well. But she'd recovered and out of her troubled past, she'd done something to make her life and the lives of others around her better. That was what forgiveness did for a person.

"Yes, she did all of those things, but she eventually got back on the right path. It just took a little forgiveness and some help to do it. Help like I needed." Christian leaned down then brushed a kiss over Joan's lips. "I love you," he whispered.

"I love you, too. You can't do this, Christian. I have an idea about what his taking your power means to the rest of the world." Joan clasped his biceps in a tight grip, seemingly unwilling to let him move away from her. "One person isn't worth the lives of millions."

"Yet I know other Enforcers who have sacrificed themselves for the ones they loved, so I'm not the only one who believes one person is more important than millions," Christian muttered.

"True, but I'm forced to point out that what they sacrificed wasn't going to give me more power," Lucifer spoke up. "They just gave up their power and souls to keep their lovers from dying. You're giving me your soul and your power to save your lover from hell. Trust me, there is a small difference."

"Shut up, Daystar," Christian ordered, not looking away from Joan. He rubbed his thumb over her bottom lip. "You don't understand what you've done for me in the time since we first met. They will all tell you that I was on the edge of becoming the very creatures I hunted. The fallen who allowed their hopelessness to overcome any part of their heart. I've felt the darkness calling to me for a century or more, and I was weakening."

Tears welled up in Joan's hazel eyes, and Christian wanted her to remember the good times, not the last moment of his life when Lucifer wrenched his power and angelic soul from him. Christian touched her forehead then caught her as she slumped.

After laying her on the couch, he turned to look at Lucifer. "Let's go to the roof. I don't want to take the chance that she'll wake up while you're sucking me dry."

Lucifer bit his lip and Christian wondered what the fallen was holding back, but again Lucifer surprised him by not saying anything. Not even the crude comment he could've made.

"Follow me then." Lucifer shimmered, then disappeared.

Christian brushed one last kiss over Joan's lips before he too dissolved. He reappeared on the roof to find Lucifer standing on top of the small wall bordering the edge. As much as he didn't want to, Christian joined him. They stared down at the bustling streets below them.

"Do you remember standing at the boundary of Heaven, and looking down at these mortals?" Lucifer's voice was soft like he was lost in memories of better days between them.

Smiling, Christian nodded. "We never could understand what He saw in them, yet we knew our job was to protect them for Him."

Lucifer sighed. "Until that moment when our lives changed forever."

"Why did you do it, Lucifer?" Christian had often asked his former friend that, but he'd always felt that the answers Lucifer gave him weren't the true ones.

"Does it matter now? You're going to die, Christian. You're going to cease to exist when I take your soul. Unlike our brethren who will find a place somewhere when they die, you'll be nothing."

"It doesn't matter. If I don't exist, then I won't know what I'm missing," he joked.

The look Lucifer shot Christian pierced his heart. He pressed his hand to his chest, trying to protect the wounded organ. This was the Lucifer he remembered. The one who felt things too deeply and cared too much about everything around him. That person had disappeared the instant he'd been banished from Heaven. He'd turned into the cynical, uncaring creature most of the fallen and mortals knew.

"Why? Please, you owe me that much, Daystar. Why did you rebel?"

"It was what he wanted," Lucifer spoke so softly, Christian almost didn't hear him.

"What who wanted?"

Christian started to reach out to touch his friend, but Lucifer cursed and shifted out of range before Christian could lay a hand on him.

"It's not important, and we need to get this done before the rest of your friends show up to try and stop me." Lucifer grabbed Christian's hand and figuratively pulled with his power, taking Christian's.

But where Christian thought it would be the most agonizing experience in his life, aside from losing his wings, there wasn't any pain. His vision went black, then there was nothing.

Lucifer sucked his breath in as Christian's power swirled around inside him for a few seconds before he could corral it. He managed to gather it and wall it away in the small part of his own soul that he had left. Closing his eyes, he refused to fall to his knees in misery for the loss of his friend, even though they hadn't been friends for millennia.

When he opened his eyes a few minutes later, he stared at the spot where Christian had stood, absently thinking that there should be a marker or something to show where one fallen angel foolishly had given up his entire existence to save one mortal, but there was nothing to show that Christian had chosen love over duty.

Running his hand over his hair, Lucifer sighed, tired to his bones. What was it about Christian, Celeste and William that made them believe in love so much that they were willing to give up any chance at returning to heaven for the mere thought of the emotion? He'd never met any mortal or angel special enough to distract him from his appointed task.

Unlike the fallen he supposedly ruled, there would never be a chance of going back home for him. He'd known the possible outcome when he'd chosen to rebel, and he couldn't whine now about the path he'd taken.

An electrical surge racing through his body warned him that the others were converging on his position. It was time to make himself scarce, yet he discovered he couldn't leave like he'd wanted. Something—or someone—was keeping him there.

When they arrived at the empty rooftop seconds later, Celeste searched for any sign of Christian and Lucifer. Mika'il knew what had happened the moment

Christian ceased to exist. He'd felt his friend's absence in his heart like a knife.

"Fuck! We're too late." Celeste looked at Mika'il. "Lucifer took Christian's soul. What the hell do we do now?"

"We pray." Mika'il shuddered as he thought about how powerful Lucifer was now, with Christian's power mingling with his own.

"Seriously? Do you think praying is going to get us out of this mess?"

He glared at her. "I don't know, Celeste. This has never happened before. I have no instructions on what to do if Lucifer were to have this much power."

"You could go and kill him. You can't allow him to wander around earth like a god." Celeste shoved her hands through her hair in frustration.

It was Mika'il's turn to show his annoyance. "I'll get right on that because I always go off on my own without any orders from the Father. I'm not a renegade angel to take justice into his own hands."

Celeste stared at him, and he could see the anger mingled with fear in her eyes. They were the same emotions rushing through him at break neck speed. This was the one thing that wasn't supposed to happen, yet it had, and they were reeling trying to find an answer to the problem.

"Guys, you seem to have forgotten something."

They both turned to look at William, who stood nearest to the edge of the roof. He frowned, but Mika'il couldn't see what was bothering William.

"What did we miss?" Celeste asked.

"If the Father didn't want this to happen, he could've stopped it at any point. He could've told Mika'il to get rid of Christian, or he could've done something to insure that Christian and Joan never met." William paced the length of the roof, hands clasped behind his back as he walked.

"Are you saying that *He* wanted this to happen?" Mika'il growled. He didn't like the idea that God might have allowed Lucifer to take Christian's soul for some unknown reason.

"It's the only way it could work," William murmured, continuing to stroll along while he thought out loud. "He is all powerful and all knowing. He must have a reason why this should happen."

"And we aren't supposed to know or question his motives. We accept what he tells us to do, and keep the faith that it'll all work out in the end." Bitterness colored Celeste's words.

Mika'il wished he could give voice to the doubt he felt about what had happened in the last couple of weeks, but he couldn't. As an archangel, he had to present a stoic front to the fallen, even if he wanted to cry his anger and anguish out to God. Would the Father hear him or answer him if he asked?

A warm breeze teased his hair, and Mika'il saw Celeste and William react to the wind as well. He lifted his chin, absorbing the way it traced his jaw and the slope of his nose. Then it seemed like it surrounded him in a tight hug. Mika'il relaxed, letting his worries go as he breathed out.

God was there, and he was good. Mika'il didn't need to know why things happened the way they did. He only had to accept that God was all-powerful and all-knowing, and that because he saw the beginning and end of time, he knew what purpose this whole situation served.

"All right. We can't do anything about what's happened, but we need to take care of Joan. She's going to feel abandoned and guilty, and we're going to have to help her work through this without climbing back into the bottle." Mika'il gestured toward the stairwell leading down to Christian's apartment.

Celeste and William sighed, but neither argued. They had to be missing their loved ones, but Mika'il couldn't stay with Joan. He had to keep track of Lucifer, to see if the fallen was taking advantage of his new powers to sow discord amongst the humans.

"Take turns if you want, or call up Danielle to come and help out. I have to go and see where Lucifer is right now." Mika'il started to focus his thoughts on Lucifer.

William went to stand next to Celeste, but before any of them could leave, Lucifer appeared on the roof before them. Smiling, he watched them tense as he stepped off the edge to walk closer to them.

"You were looking for me?" Lucifer looked at Mika'il, and winked.

Mika'il gritted his teeth. He wouldn't let the fallen bait him. Mostly because Lucifer always seemed to enjoy it when he got Mika'il worked up.

"I was, actually. I wanted to make sure you weren't suffering any ill effects from the infusion of power you received after taking Christian's."

He wanted to wipe off the smirk marring Lucifer's face. Even with the cross burnt into his left cheek, Lucifer was the most beautiful creature Mika'il had ever seen. Yet it was a shattered beauty that made Mika'il want to weep every time he saw him.

Lucifer held his arms out to the sides. "You can check, my friend, but trust me, I'm doing fine. And please don't worry about your dear mortals. I have no plans on harming them." He paused for a moment, then continued, "Tonight anyway."

Mika'il realized that was the only concession he was going to receive from Lucifer. He studied the most powerful fallen on earth, and he noticed, hidden amongst the arrogance and pride in Lucifer's eyes, there was a hint of sadness as well.

He'd never imagined Lucifer would feel sad about what he'd done to Christian. Yet in a way, Mika'il shouldn't have been shocked by that emotion either because at one time, Lucifer and Christian had been close friends—almost as close as Mika'il and Lucifer had been. While he might not care about any of the other fallen he'd led astray, Lucifer had cared about Christian.

"He was my friend at one time as well, Mika'il. No matter how we felt about each other now, I always carry the memory of what we once were to each other. Just as I carry the memory of our friendship." Lucifer bowed his head in Mika'il's direction.

"If you honored your friendship with Christian, why did you take him up on his offer? Why didn't you walk away?" Celeste spoke up, unable to continue listening to Lucifer's bullshit.

The pitying look Lucifer shot Celeste annoyed Mika'il for some reason. The person who deserved pity was Lucifer because he'd lost all hope of ever returning to Heaven. At least Celeste would be going home when she died because of her love for Adam. Mika'il opened his mouth, ready to berate Lucifer when the fallen shook his head.

"It doesn't work that way, Celeste. I know you have no experience with bargaining with the devil, but trust me, once a deal is set, no one can renege on it." Lucifer sighed, and the pain in that sound caused Mika'il to blink. "No matter how much one might wish they could."

"But you're the one who made the rules," William pointed out.

Lucifer chuckled. "Where did you get that foolish idea? I set no rules or agendas. It wasn't any of my doing."

After whirling around, Lucifer dashed to the edge of the building, but before he jumped, he turned to look at them. "Don't worry about Joan. Something tells me she'll be all right, and she'll find her love again."

He leaped to the top of the brick wall forming the edge of the roof. Spreading his arms wide, Lucifer stared up into the dark night sky, and Mika'il was reminded of another holy being who'd assumed that position to save mortals. Then Lucifer stepped off and disappeared into thin air with a small hiss to mark his passing.

William looked at Celeste and him. "What did he mean, Joan'll find her love again?"

Mika'il shrugged as he mentally acknowledged a silent order to leave as it passed through his mind. "I don't know. I try very hard not to get caught up in Lucifer's riddles. I have to go. Something is happening in Los Angeles that needs my attention. Keep an eye on Joan for a couple of days. If it looks like she's handling this all right, then you have my permission to return to your homes."

He turned, allowing himself a little bit of whining about having to go so quickly. He'd like to have stayed to chat with Celeste and William when there wasn't some kind of mortal-threatening problem happening. Mika'il didn't have many friends, considering he spent a great deal of his time with mortals and the fallen—far more time than he spent with the other angels and heavenly creatures.

As he left, Mika'il sent a prayer to the Father that Joan would be able to stay strong, and that she'd be able to love again after losing Christian that day.

"Trust me, Mika'il."

"I do, my Lord. In all things, but sometimes even I can't see the good in something like this," he admitted.

"You don't have to, because I can, and that's the most important thing."

He bowed to God's admonishment, then turned his thoughts to Los Angeles and the next situation he had to deal with. One involving Cassandra, and a certain transplanted Chicago homicide detective. *This one could be interesting,* he thought as he allowed his power to overtake him.

Chapter Eight

"It's time."

Christian glanced over to where Lucifer stood, hands on hips and a slight smile on his face. After standing, Christian strolled over and studied him.

"Time for what?"

"For you to go back," Lucifer informed him.

Christian couldn't believe what he'd heard. "Go back? But I gave up my power and my soul for Joan. There's no going back from that."

"Usually there isn't, but you and Joan aren't the usual couple. I'm sending you back, but there is a catch."

"There's always a catch with you, Lucifer, but if you send me back, I'll forgive you everything that you've ever done to me." Christian wanted to see Joan again so badly. The entire time he'd been wherever Lucifer had sent him, all he'd been able to think about was Joan.

"You won't remember what happened to you. You'll think you went out to Los Angeles on orders from Mika'il, and that you've only been gone for a week."

Lucifer shifted from foot to foot, obviously wanting to get on with the whole thing.

"Will I have my power back?"

Lucifer nodded. "Of course you will. I don't need it, no matter what the hell I tell people."

Christian reached out to take Lucifer's hand, but the fallen stepped away so that Christian couldn't touch him.

"Thank you, Lucifer. I wish things were different between us and we could go back to being friends."

"Maybe someday God will forgive us both," Lucifer murmured as he pressed his fingertip to Christian's forehead.

* * * *

Joan bent over, placing her hands on her knees while trying to catch her breath. She worked on not collapsing as her heart rate slowed down. It was a nice warm, mild day in October, and she'd taken advantage of the weather to go for a run in Central Park.

As she walked around in a small circle across from the park entrance closest to her apartment building, a striking man standing about five feet from her caught her attention. In many ways, he reminded her of Christian, but she knew he was gone. The man she'd loved had given up his soul to keep her from the devil, and his sacrifice had convinced Joan she'd been right to love him.

The man noticed her staring, and she quickly dropped her gaze to the ground in front of her. Yet she sensed he was approaching her. When a pair of highly polished Italian leather dress shoes came into her line of vision, she grimaced, then raised her head to meet his dark stare. There was something so familiar about him, like she'd known him a long time ago.

Intense black eyes studied her, almost seeming to cut right to her soul. Joan gasped when he reached out to caress her cheek. Jerking away from the stranger, she glared.

His smile softened his sculpted beauty into something more human. She wondered at the cross-shaped scar on his left cheek. *Where would such a man as seemingly sophisticated as this one get a wound like that?*

"He loved you so much, Joan, and I can see why. Even after all you've gone through, your soul is still pure." His voice sounded like the ringing of the bells at St. Patrick's cathedral in New York City.

Yet tears welled in Joan's eyes because there was such terrible sadness running as undercurrents in the music of his voice. She wanted to wrap her arms around him, bring him close to her heart, and tell him that whatever made him so sad would ease in time.

As if he were reading her mind, he laughed softly. "I'm sorry, my dear. There will be no easing of my pain, but I didn't come here for that. I think you've been alone long enough. Your future will start tonight, and I promise it'll be far brighter than your past."

Before she could ask what he meant, the man disappeared. Joan blinked before looking around to see if she could find him in the crowd, but he was nowhere to be found. *How in the world can any mortal man move that fast?*

Just as she finished thinking that, another thought jumped into her head. *Maybe he wasn't mortal. He knew about Christian, and he looked familiar, like someone I knew a long time ago.*

Taking a deep breath, Joan let the encounter settled into her, and tried not to freak out. There was a lingering scent of cinnamon, and she knew it hadn't come from her. Nothing had happened, except that he'd touched her. She pressed her fingers to the exact spot where the stranger's had rested, imagining she still felt his touch.

She shook off any worries or fears, not having time to deal with it. She needed to get home and showered before leaving to meet Lisa for dinner and a night on the town. It was the first time she was going out since that night. Joan found she was excited about it, knowing Christian wouldn't have wanted her to become a hermit and mourn him the rest of her life.

Joan would celebrate the life he died to give her, and she'd raise a glass of sparkling water in his memory tonight.

* * * *

"May I buy you a water?"

The minute the man's voice spoke those words, Joan whirled around. She gasped when she saw Christian standing there, just as gorgeous as he'd been the day they'd met. Joan flung herself into his arms as he grinned at her.

"Oh, my God! Christian, how are you here?" She pressed her lips to his ear to be heard over the music.

"Where else would I be? I'm sorry I didn't call to let you know I'd be home tonight, but it took a little while longer for me to finish the job." He leaned down to brush a kiss over her cheek.

"A job?"

Was he serious? What job? Lucifer had taken his soul, and he'd died. Celeste and William hadn't been able to tell Joan where Christian had gone, but they had said he was gone, never to return. Yet here he stood.

"Yes. Mika'il needed me to go to Los Angeles to check on a mutual friend." He pulled her close to nuzzle her jaw.

"Do you know what you are?" She couldn't believe that Christian was there.

Christian pulled away from her to meet her gaze as he frowned. "What I am? Do you want to discuss that while we're standing here in the middle of a club?"

She shook her head. "How about we head home? I'd like to say hello properly."

Not wanting to get caught into a conversation with Lisa and her other friends, she pulled out her phone to send Lisa a quick text. After tucking it back into her clutch, she slid her arm through Christian's and smiled at him.

"Let's go home," she said.

He led her from the club then flagged down a cab to take them back, not to her house but to his. Joan didn't know what to say. She was stunned that Christian was sitting next to her in the vehicle, and she kept her fingers entwined with his, afraid that if she let go, he'd disappear on her.

Why is he back? And he remembers everything except maybe what happened with Lucifer. She wanted to call Celeste and ask her what was going on, but she had the strange feeling that the other fallen wouldn't know any more about it than Joan did.

Once they got inside Christian's penthouse, Christian wrapped his arms around her, brought her close to him then kissed her. Joan had so many questions, but she wanted Christian more than answers.

She buried her fingers in his blond hair, holding him tight while soaking up his familiar scent and the feel of his body against hers. Underneath his musky scent was another one that reminded her of the man she'd met earlier that day.

Before Joan could think anything more about that, Christian reached down to push up the hem of her dress. It was obvious he wasn't interested in taking the time to get naked. He walked her back toward the couch in the middle of his living room.

Joan didn't fight him, just relaxed into his embrace and let him lead. He lowered her onto the cushions then settled between her thighs. He hooked his fingers through the strap of her thong before ripping it off her. She gasped while her desire grew. He'd never been so rough with her, but Joan wasn't worried. There wasn't any way he'd ever hurt her.

He met her shocked gaze. "I'm sorry but this going to be fast and rough. I need you too much, love."

She cradled his face in her hands. "It's all right. I can handle whatever you give me. I want you, Christian. It's been so lonely without you."

"Without me? I've only been gone for a week." Christian frowned.

Joan didn't want to talk about it right there. She dropped her hands to the belt on Christian's slacks, fumbling to open it. Christian helped her get his pants down to his knees before pressing between her legs.

Their breath mingled as they each sighed while he sank into her. It didn't matter that they were still dressed. She wrapped her legs around his waist then lifted her hips to bring him even farther in.

"Joan," Christian groaned as he began to thrust slowly and easily at first as if he was learning her body all over again.

She bit her lip as his cock brushed over the spot inside her. Each stroke in brought their bodies together in the most primitive way, and she loved how it felt to be filled by him. Joan wanted to be claimed by him again. For him it might have only been a week, but for her, it had been a month, and she'd thought she'd never see him again.

Christian slipped his hand between them to rub over her clit, driving her closer and closer to the edge. Staring up into Christian's blue eyes, she saw all of his love for her in them. She hoped he could see the same in hers because she loved him with all her heart, and she thanked God for letting him come back.

Her orgasm slammed over her and she cried out, "Christian!"

He rocked faster and harder into her as he lost all of his rhythm. Her clenching inner muscles massaged his length as she shuddered. Christian thrust deep, then froze as his own climax hit him. His head fell forward, and he groaned as he flooded her with his cum.

Joan let her legs drop to the sides, but encircled Christian's shoulders to hold him as he collapsed on top of her. She pressed her face to his sweat-covered hair as she tried to calm her own breathing.

When he grunted, she figured he had recovered enough to move, so Joan pinched his side.

"What?" He pushed up on his elbows to stare at her.

"I think we should go clean up, then talk about what happened."

Christian frowned. "What happened?"

"Let's just do it, and I'll tell you."

"Okay."

She shivered as his softened cock slid from her when he rolled over to kneel next to the couch. Christian pushed to his feet, then tugged up his pants but didn't bother buttoning them. Joan took the hand he offered her and smiled as he easily pulled her to her feet.

Once they got into his shower, she leaned against him while the warm water cascaded over her. She sighed as he washed her everywhere, even between her legs though she tried to stop him from doing that.

Christian pressed his lips to her hand as he looked up at her from where he crouched on the tiled floor. "Let me take care of you. I've missed you."

"All right."

She let him take charge of her again, not wanting to argue with him, though she knew the upcoming conversation was going to be interesting. Since Christian didn't seem to have any memory of what had happened, she imagined he would be hard to convince.

Eventually they were seated at the island in his kitchen. He was cooking them some spaghetti while she sipped water from a crystal glass. Now that she wasn't caught up in seeing him again or flat on her back being fucked by him, she noticed something on his chest.

"What's that on your chest?"

Christian glanced down then turned to show her. "It's my tattoo. You've seen it before. I've had it for several years."

Joan shook her head. "I don't remember seeing it before, and considering how much sex we've had, I would think I would've seen it."

She crooked her finger to have him come closer. When he stopped right in front of her, she ran her fingers over the phoenix tattooed on his chest. It was beautiful work, but faded like it had been done a few years ago. Joan frowned, knowing Christian hadn't had anything like that before Lucifer took him.

"All right. I think we need to talk about some things." She pointed at the stove. "That's done, isn't it?"

"Yes." He dished out the late night supper, then joined her. They ate in silence for a little bit before Christian wiped his mouth with his napkin, then glanced at her. "Tell me what's going on. Why are you acting strange?"

Joan shook her head. "Christian, you've been gone over a month."

His eyes widened in shock. "You're joking. I was in Los Angeles working with Nevan and Cassandra for a week. Not a month."

She shook her head. "No. Do you remember what you are?"

"I'm the head Enforcer for the entire East Coast. As such, I'm the second most powerful fallen, and only Lucifer is stronger than me," he recited his credentials like he thought she'd lost her mind.

"Christian, you've been gone for over a month, not a week like you think." Joan knew she was going to have to call Celeste or William to totally convince him, but she had to try on her own first.

"I was only needed for a week until Cassandra got control of the situation. Mika'il told me I could come home."

She narrowed her eyes. Was the archangel responsible for Christian's return? Too bad she didn't feel confident enough to demand his presence. Of course, most people wouldn't dare to demand a meeting with one of the top creatures in heaven.

"A month ago, Lucifer was about to take my soul, but you offered yours instead. No way was he going to pass that up, so he took it." She reached out to trace the edges of the phoenix's wings. "Now here you stand—a phoenix rising from the ashes or wherever you've been. Somehow he let you come back to me."

Christian frowned. "If what you say is true, Lucifer would never allow me to come back to you. I should be trapped somewhere, or non-existent. Lucifer isn't the type of creature who would feel sympathy and allow me to return to you simply because you missed me."

A flash of memory raced through Joan's brain, and she gasped. "That's why you smell like him," she murmured.

"Smell like who? You're really not making any sense, Joan. Have you started drinking again?"

Rearing back, she glared at him. "No I haven't been drinking again, jackass. Early today I was out jogging in Central Park, and this man approached me. I didn't know who he was, but he was beautiful and had a cross-shaped scar on his left cheek."

Christian growled. "He's supposed to stay away from you."

"He didn't do anything except touch my cheek, Christian. Trust me, he wasn't interested in hurting me. He told me that I'd been alone long enough, and that my future would start tonight. Lucifer must have decided at some point to let you come back to me. And you smell like cinnamon, which he did as well, so you must have been with him at some point. But why didn't I recognize him from before?"

"He probably wiped your memory of him. For whatever reason he didn't want you to remember what he looked like when he came to see you for the last time."

Christian still didn't look convinced, but Joan discovered she didn't care. All that mattered was that Christian was back with her, seemingly whole and in love with her. That was all she cared about. She decided they had done enough talking for one night.

* * * *

Mika'il stood at Ground Zero, staring up at One World Trade Center. He thought about the resilience of mortals, of how they always came back from tragedy stronger than they'd been before.

A strange combination of sulfur and cinnamon filled the air, and Mika'il knew Lucifer had joined him. He didn't turn to look at him, just kept his gaze on the new building.

Finally he asked, "Why did you do it?"

"I wasn't there for that. Not all the evil humans do to each other can be placed on my shoulders. Free will plays a part."

Mika'il huffed in annoyance. Lucifer was being deliberately obtuse.

"You know what I meant. Why did you let Christian come back?"

Lucifer didn't say anything for several minutes, and if Mika'il hadn't been able to feel his presence, he'd have assumed Lucifer had disappeared. Just as Mika'il was going to ask again, Lucifer spoke.

"Christian had served his purpose," Lucifer informed him.

"What purpose was that?" It was Mika'il's turn to play the innocent.

Lucifer grunted in amusement. "Innocence doesn't show well on you, Mika'il. I know what he has you doing, and Christian's death was part of that overall plan."

Mika'il didn't confirm or deny Lucifer's statements, though he turned to look at Lucifer. The fallen angel had his head tilted back, and moonlight seemed to caress the cross branded on Lucifer's cheek.

"You still haven't answered me," he persisted.

Lucifer began to fade, but his next comment lingered in Mika'il's thoughts for months to come.

"The reason I let him come back is my own, and it might not be what you assume it to be."

LOS ANGELES

Dedication

We've all encountered angels in our lives who lift us
up and show us a better life.

Chapter One

"God works in mysterious ways," Cassandra murmured as she stepped out from the back of her car.

"Ma'am?" The young uniformed officer sounded like he wasn't sure how to answer her. Tommy had sent him to meet her when she arrived and she was pretty sure he hadn't explained to the man why she needed a driver.

"Nothing." She smiled at him while standing just outside the crime scene. She waited for Kaiser to join her before moving in the direction of all the noise. "Where do you think Tommy is?"

There was no answer. Of course there wouldn't be. Kaiser was an amazing Seeing Eye Dog, but he couldn't talk. Though he did know Tommy, and he'd take her to him if he could find him. As she approached, the din separated into individual sounds. Some of which she recognized and some she didn't.

"You're not allowed in there." A voice as smooth as the finest brandy filled her ear and a shiver raced down Cassandra's spine to rest in the pit of her stomach. "It's an active crime scene. We can't have you or your dog contaminating it."

She tilted her head up, knowing from the direction of his words that he was taller than her. The clipped tones said he was ticked off about something. Also, the looming darkness she sensed radiating off him.

"I'd like to talk to Detective Davidson."

"He's in the middle of a case. Call him later at the station." He moved away from her.

He had dismissed her and anger surged inside her. Was it because she was a woman or because she was blind? Cassandra would've loved to read his mind, but she tried to stay away from that trap. After reaching into her pocket, she pulled out her phone.

She hit the button and heard, "Hello, Cassandra."

"Call Tommy," she spoke clearly.

"Davidson." Tommy's high-pitched voice squeaked in her ear.

"Hey. I'm outside. One of your guys wouldn't let me in." She gave a little tug on Kaiser's harness and he led her away from the group to a quiet place where she wouldn't bother anyone.

"What'd he look like?"

She smiled—the fact she couldn't see never stopped Tommy from treating her like a normal person. "He was tall. His voice was smooth, but he didn't feel happy to me. Plus he's from Chicago."

"Must have been my new partner. Largent worked homicide in Chicago for a while. Got shot and decided to move out West. The Sheriff hired him last week. I'll send Johnson out for you."

"Thanks." Cassandra dropped the phone in her pocket. So he had been injured. That would explain the hint of pain she'd heard hidden in his voice.

Kaiser whined and she knelt to wrap her arms around the large Rhodesian Ridgeback. "Sorry, old man. You can't come in with me. All your dog hair will contaminate the scene. We don't want the new detective hunting us down. Take me back to the police car."

They returned to the car then she opened the back door for Kaiser to jump in. "I'll be back in a few minutes."

"Miss Harmen," a hesitant voice came from behind her.

Johnson had being standing there for a few minutes. She'd sensed his presence as he walked up. "Yes, Officer Johnson?"

"I'm supposed to escort you to Detective Davidson."

"I'll need to take your arm, Officer. My guide dog can't go in." She reached out and he threaded her arm through his.

His emotions bombarded her. He was nervous about her, having heard the rumors going around the station. A lot of the deputies didn't know how she solved the cases she worked on. Most of them assumed she had some connection to the criminal underground and that's where she got her information.

Cassandra smiled. If any of them knew the truth, they'd probably lock her up as delusional. Being a fallen angel was bad enough, but being blind as well had become overwhelming after centuries. She used to be able to see then she'd been injured in the seventeen hundreds, and for some reason, her healing ability had deserted her.

When she'd asked Mika'il about it, he'd had no explanation or reason as to why it had happened. Maybe it was another form of punishment from God.

She hadn't believed that was true then the visions had started, and she'd formed the opinion she was in hell. Cassandra had always imagined the worst that could happen was her wings were taken, but she should've known thinking that tempted fate to prove her wrong.

"Hey, I said you couldn't come in here." The seductive voice of Detective Largent teased her again as his presence loomed over her.

Johnson's arm trembled under her hand. She tried not to read the officer's mind, but his thoughts projected strong enough that she couldn't stop them from coming through. Even though he was new, Largent was getting the reputation of being hard-nosed and driven. The young man was remembering how Largent had chewed him out for not filling a report properly.

"Good thing you're not the lead on this case, Detective." She turned away from Largent. "Take me to Detective Davidson, Officer."

She could feel that Largent wanted to say something, but he didn't have control over who Davidson allowed in. He followed them to where Davidson waited.

"Hey, beautiful. Why is it you get better looking every time I see you and I just get uglier?" Davidson touched her shoulder to warn her before he hugged her.

Even though he joked with her, there was a current of worry underlying his words.

"Good genes, I guess. Of course I think you're lying about getting uglier." Cassandra allowed herself to accept his embrace. Touching people wasn't something she enjoyed. Their emotions tended to swamp her at times, even when she had her walls up as high as she could get them.

"What's she doing here, Davidson?" Largent snarled.

"She's here because she'll tell us if there's been a crime. Let me explain, Cassandra." Davidson took a deep breath. "We think the occupant of this house was involved in a crime, but we have no proof."

"Then why are you here? Without any proof, you can't enter the premises, can you?"

"Not usually but a family member allowed us in. They were worried about the home owner as well." Davidson tucked her hand in the crook of his arm. "I want you to look at the house. I'll be right behind you."

Cassandra took a deep breath. She hated the first traumatic punch hitting her when she entered a crime scene. She gave a small sigh when the first couple of rooms were devoid of any feeling of violence or hatred. Well, except for the distrust rolling off Largent as he stalked behind them.

Stepping into the next room, she doubled over as the pain hit her. The vision in her mind showed the walls and floor covered with blood. Reaching out, she grabbed a hold of Largent's arm. She jerked away as an electric shock raced through her body.

"Tommy, have CSI come through here. Take up the carpet as well. You'll find your proof."

Largent escorted her back outside without saying a word while Davidson ordered the crime scene people in. They stood quietly for a minute or two while she tried to collect her thoughts. Cassandra appreciated him not talking, though she could almost hear his disapproval. She sensed a large object in front of her and put her hand out to touch it. It was the police car.

"Am I close to the back door of the cruiser?"

"Yes."

She opened it and Kaiser brushed her hand as he jumped out. Scratching his ears, she listened to the people around her. "You're the relative," she told Detective Largent.

His jerk told her she was right.

"How did you figure that out?"

"In my vision, the blood I saw was connected to you."

"I didn't do it." Anger clipped his words.

She shook her head. "Of course you didn't. A line of energy connected you with whoever lived in the house. It could only happen if you were related."

Largent took a deep breath. "You said lived."

Cassandra rested her hand on his arm. "I'm sorry, but they're dead. It was their blood I saw." An odd feeling washed over her. "You knew that. How?"

His arm moved and she imagined he shrugged. "Just a hunch. My cousin, Patrick. He was reclusive and eccentric. No one in the family had heard from him for a while. Since I moved out here, I checked up on him."

"Was he into the occult?"

"He thought our family descended from a Druid high priest. He believed in magic."

"And you don't?" She didn't believe that.

Largent chuckled. "Let's say I'm trying to keep an open mind about it."

A car pulling up and the whirring of a window rolling down caught her attention. "Cassandra, are you done here?"

Davidson must have called her driver to come and pick her up. "For now, Eli."

Kaiser led her to the car, and she found the door handle. She had her dog jump up before she turned back to look in Largent's direction. "It's hard to believe you're pretending to keep an open mind about the paranormal when you've been touched by it."

He grunted like she'd punched him and she smiled while climbing in to the car. After shutting the door, she leaned back against the seat with a sigh. "Take me home, Eli."

"Well, I'm actually supposed to take you to the Cathedral of Our Lady of Angels before you go home." Eli didn't sound happy about it.

"And why are you supposed to do that?" There were two creatures in the world that could order Eli to do anything. The true demon that had appointed himself her guardian didn't take orders well, and certainly not from any human or Fallen.

"Who do you think?" He put the car in gear and they left the crime scene.

She grimaced as she stroked Kaiser's head where he'd laid it in her lap. "We don't have a choice. If we don't go, he'll come looking for us and I hate when he invades my house."

Eli's snort made her smile. He hated getting visits from the archangel even more than she did. Of course, Mika'il had spent thousands of years hunting and destroying Eli's kind. It was hard for him not to hold a grudge against him.

"Why don't you relax? Getting those visions take a lot out of you."

Leaning her head back against the cushion, she closed her eyes. It was strange that that simple act was enough to ease the tension from her muscles. The darkness didn't change or get deeper with her eyes shut or anything like that, yet it was something normal to do. Not that her life had ever been normal.

Cassandra let go for a little while. Eli would get her to the cathedral in one piece and she could deal with

Mika'il when she got there. No point in getting upset beforehand.

"Good idea, Cassandra. I get the feeling the next couple of weeks will be exhausting."

She stiffened as the other person she didn't want to see or talk to invaded her head. *"Lucifer. What do you want?"*

"Nothing. Just to give you a friendly warning. Things are happening in the city that intrigue me."

Rolling her eyes didn't have the same effect when there wasn't anyone there to see her do it. *"Things are always happening here, but it must be strange to intrigue you. Nothing excites you anymore. Am I going to have to worry about you interfering or can I just deal with Mika'il on this?"*

Lucifer's laugh rang through her head like the purest bells on a clear day. *"Worry about the archangel for now, Cassandra. I'll be in touch."*

"That's what I'm afraid of," she muttered after his presence had left her mind.

"What?"

"Nothing, Eli. Just talking to myself."

Any hope of resting before meeting up with Mika'il was gone. She turned to face the window, wishing for the thousandth time she could see the city as it passed by.

* * * *

Nevan Largent tossed his keys on the kitchen counter as he walked into his house. Cassandra had been right. When the techs did their job, the walls had lit up in huge blood splatter patterns, plus there had been old symbols painted in older dried blood on the walls and floors.

Standing there, he stared at the phone. When he'd left Chicago, he had vowed never to contact anyone from there. But he needed information and there was one person who he knew could help him. With a huff of annoyance, he picked up the phone then dialed.

"Hello?"

"Grant, it's Largent."

"Well, well, if it isn't our favorite detective. What apocalyptic event happened to make you call us?" Grant's voice filled with sarcasm.

"Is Danielle there? I need to talk to her."

"Sure."

He could hear Grant call for Danielle, and Nevan was glad that when it came to these situations, Grant didn't display any curiosity. Knowing fallen angels existed and all those legends were true was more than enough for Danielle's man.

"Nevan."

"Hello, Danielle. How are you doing?"

"We're surviving, considering Lucifer took Christian's soul last week." Sadness and worry colored her words.

Nevan wasn't privy to most of what went on in the world of fallen angels and the ones they hunted, but even he knew that wasn't a good thing. "Is there anything Mika'il can do?"

Danielle cleared her throat. "No. We just have to wait and see what Lucifer does with all that power."

Well, after hearing that, his problem didn't seem all that serious. He considered not asking Danielle for help and just hanging up.

"What can I do for you, Nevan?"

"I need some help."

There was no hesitation. "I can get a flight out and be there tomorrow afternoon."

Her willingness to come without knowing what he needed touched him, especially after he'd acted like such an ass every time he dealt with her in Chicago. "Just information right now. What can you tell me about the occult and druids?"

She thought for a moment. "Is this about your cousin?"

"Yes. He's been murdered, or at least I think he has. We haven't found his body, but there were occult symbols at the murder scene." He didn't like the idea of having to purposefully enter the world he'd run from most of his life.

"I can check around and see if I can get you a name of someone you can talk to out there. I'm sorry." Her voice went soft.

"I know."

"If there wasn't a body, how did you find out about the murder? Did you see something?"

Shaking his head even though she couldn't see him, Nevan said, "I brought my partner in when Patrick didn't answer my phone calls or the door when I went to check on him. We couldn't find anything, so Davidson called in this woman he works with." He didn't want to say anything, but he knew he couldn't hide it from her. "She's one of you."

"One of me? Oh, you mean a fallen angel." Danielle hummed under her breath for a second. "I guess she could be. I don't know everyone who lives out there. What was her name?"

"Cassandra. I didn't get her last name. She's blind, which is weird. Can't your kind heal from just about any kind of injury?"

"For the most part, yes. Her name doesn't sound familiar, but while I'm looking to find someone for you to talk to, I'll see if I can get some information on her as well. She's psychic?"

Nevan strolled over to his fridge to check what kind of food he had. "I don't know. Is it what we call psychic ability or is it because of her being a fallen?"

"Good question. I'll have to do some research on this."

"I think she knows about me. She said I was touched by the paranormal."

Danielle laughed. "You can't get away from being a sensitive just because you're uncomfortable with it. Being a fallen, she'd know you had abilities even if she wasn't blind. You chose to be one before you were born, Nevan. Deal with it and use it."

"How soon can you get me those names?" He wasn't interested in discussing his talents at the moment.

"I'll email them to you in the morning."

"Thank you, Danielle. I owe you." He stared at the containers of leftovers, wondering if he had enough energy to heat them up.

"Just be happy, Nevan. That's all I want for you."

After hanging up, he stuffed his phone back in his pocket then pulled out a Tupperware dish. He checked to make sure it was still good before he popped it in the microwave. While waiting, he leaned against the counter and stared at the floor.

"What were you into, Patrick? Why couldn't you have left well enough alone?" Nevan clenched his hands. "Did you want this curse so badly that you would've sacrificed for it?"

Unfortunately, his cousin couldn't answer him. Nevan's head shot up when a thought hit him. He could see the dead and spirits caught in the mortal world. Those who were murdered tended to hang around because of the violence committed against them. Yet there hadn't been anything in Patrick's house.

Had Patrick been injured in the house, then taken elsewhere and killed? Was that why his spirit wasn't there? Or could something else have been done to him? He'd have to wait until he got Danielle's email before he could proceed. At least Nevan had Davidson to help him find out who had killed Patrick and why.

Nevan had a sneaking suspicion he wasn't going to be thrilled when he found out the truth. The microwave dinged and he removed his dinner. After grabbing a fork, he wandered into the living room then flopped on the couch.

There had to be a football game on some channel. He'd watch TV and eat before taking a shower and going to bed. He hoped they didn't catch another dead body. A good night's rest would help him focus in the morning.

* * * *

Later on that night, shadows crawled across Nevan's bedroom floor as he tossed and turned under the covers. Voices whispered in his ear, waking him up and keeping him from falling back asleep. After sitting up, he swung his feet over the side of the bed. He braced his elbows on his knees before resting his face in his hands.

He could still hear words in the silence surrounding him but he didn't glance around. Spirits gathered as he tried to shake the fog from his mind. Nevan tried to grab some control of his gift. He didn't want to see any of them. All he wished was to sleep through one night without being awakened by talking and cold air hovering over him.

Shoving to his feet, Nevan propped his hands on his hips while taking a deep breath. He didn't look anywhere except the door as he stalked toward it.

"I'm so fucking tired of all this shit," he muttered, wandering to the kitchen. He'd left the light over the sink on so he didn't have to fumble around to grab a glass out of the cupboard. After pouring some milk, he stood at the sink to drink it and stared out of the window into the backyard.

Once he'd focused his wandering attention on the lawn, his glass dropped into the sink, shattering. He was dimly aware of avoiding the spilt milk and the shards of glass as he raced back to his bedroom where he kept his spare gun in the nightstand drawer. He grabbed it then dashed out the back door.

Whirling in a circle, he glanced at the house then at the spot where he'd seen the man. Well, he assumed it was a man, though he couldn't be sure since he was dressed in a white robe with a hood tugged over his face. But there was no one there anymore.

"Where the hell did he go?" Nevan went inside to find a flashlight then searched every inch of his yard, but found no footprints or evidence anyone except him had been there.

After returning to the kitchen, he cleaned up the mess before wandering into the living room. Nevan flopped into the chair in the corner, holding his gun in his lap. His back against the wall, he decided to stay up for a while.

* * * *

"Damn!" The high priest stalked from one end of the altar room to the other. His rage rolled from him in waves, causing his followers to cringe.

"We brought you the one you asked for." The boldest—or most foolish—stated.

"I know you did, but he was the wrong one."

"The wrong one? But he had the blood line you were looking for." The followers looked at each other.

"Yes, but he didn't have the gift. The blood is only useful to me if it carries the gift." He tossed his hands in the air. "What do we do now? It took me years to find him."

"Sir." One of the quieter members stepped forward.

"What?" He rounded on him, glaring.

"There is another of the same blood line in the area. I've heard whispers of his uncanny abilities. He might be the one you want."

"Find out all you can about him. If he has the gift, our time might be closer than we think." He motioned for them to leave.

His followers bowed before slipping away. They separated in the labyrinth outside the altar room. They didn't know each other and never saw each other's face. They were believers searching for power.

The high priest waited until he was alone before stripping out of his robe. He knelt in front of the altar and bowed his head. He started chanting softly, letting the words slide off his tongue. The sound of it grew until it echoed throughout the chamber. He fell into a trance and the purpose behind his plans became clearer the longer he concentrated.

Chapter Two

Nevan swore when he saw the name of the expert Danielle had found for him. "I should've known," he said and Tommy looked at him from where he sat at his desk next to Nevan.

"Known what?"

"Who the hell is Cassandra Harmen? Why bring her to the house?" Nevan didn't want to talk about the other thing he'd found out that morning.

Tommy leaned far enough back in his chair to make it creak, threatening to collapse. "I've worked with her on a couple of cold cases that came across my desk. Figured if anyone could give us some leads or even let us know for sure a crime had happened, she could."

"The sheriff's okay with you using a psychic?" He couldn't help the skepticism coloring his voice, considering how his captain back in Chicago would've reacted if he'd broached the subject of a psychic.

"He never said me I couldn't do it and trust me, if he was against it, he would've let me know." Tommy twirled a pencil in his fingers. "Plus it's California, man. You know we're a little different out here."

That's an understatement. Yawning, Nevan stretched then noticed Tommy studying him. "What?"

"You look like shit, Largent. Didn't you sleep last night?" Before Nevan could say anything, Tommy continued, "I'm sorry about your cousin. It sucks knowing something bad went down, but not being able to find out what it was."

Nevan pursed his lips then shrugged. "Yeah, I couldn't get my mind to stop thinking about crap. Having to wait for all the lab results come in is going to drive me crazy." Biting the bullet, he asked, "Do you think Ms Harmen might know something more?"

Tommy screwed his face into a thoughtful expression. "She might, though usually she calls me if she gets anything else."

"Would you have a problem if I contact her?" Nevan needed to talk to her, but he wasn't going to step on Tommy's toes to do it.

He watched as Tommy grabbed a pad of paper then scribbled something on it, catching the note when Tommy tossed it at him. "Go ahead. She might not answer because she's working right now."

"Where does she work?" Nevan ripped the phone number off the pad before tossing it back to Tommy. He wouldn't think Cassandra would have to work anywhere. He knew Danielle did because—as she explained it—she had all this knowledge stored up, why not use it?

"There's a woman's shelter downtown. She can give you the address if she wants you to meet her there. Most of the time, she sets up a meeting somewhere else. The women at the shelter don't like men." Tommy gave Nevan a knowing look.

Nevan nodded, showing he understood what Tommy meant. Most of the women who went to shelters were there because of men. They were usually domestic abuse survivors or running from the very people who should be protecting them.

"I'll call her and wherever she wants, I'll go." Nevan grabbed his phone before standing. "I'm going to the coffee shop on the corner. Do you want anything?"

Tommy shook his head. "Nah. I need to call the lab about one of our other cases. There might have been a break in it, so when you get back, we'll have to take off to talk to a witness."

"I won't take long."

He left the building to wander down the sidewalk to where the coffee shop was located. To his surprise, there wasn't a big line, so he got his order right away then sat at one of the tables to call Cassandra.

"Hello?"

"Ms Harmen, this is Detective Nevan Largent. We met last night under unfortunate circumstances."

Cassandra hummed for a second. "Right. You're the one from Chicago who has the gift."

Nevan glanced around, making sure there wasn't anyone close to him. "And you're a fallen angel. I didn't know you could go blind."

Stunned silence filled the connection before Cassandra cleared her throat. "How did you know?"

"I have the gift, remember? Also, I've dealt with your kind while I was in Chicago," he admitted.

"My kind?" Cassandra sounded rather put out by that.

Nevan gritted his teeth, but he realized he could've stated things a little more diplomatically. "Fallen angels and Enforcers. Is that what you are?"

"Yes to both. You were in Chicago." Cassandra stopped for a minute then said, "I'm working right now. Can we meet somewhere and you can ask me what you want to know?"

"Fine with me. Where and when?" He didn't have a problem going wherever she wanted him to go. It was important for figuring out what happened to Patrick and to find out more about druids.

He could hear her breathing on the other end of the line while she seemed to be thinking about where to meet. Finally, she said, "As much as I hate this, I'm going to ask you to meet me at my house. Around six?"

"I can do that."

"Do you need my address?"

He chuckled. "I wouldn't be much of a detective if I couldn't get it."

Her laughter was bright and he tried not to think about how his body reacted to the sound. *Shit!* He didn't want to be attracted to the fallen angel. Thinking about wrinkly old men parading around in Speedos helped calm his cock down.

"That's true, Detective Largent. Well, I need to get going. I'll see you at six." She hung up before he could say anything.

"Goodbye, Ms Harmen," he muttered then dropped his phone in his pocket. After scooping up his coffee, he got a refill before heading back to the station.

Tommy was waiting for him and they went out to talk to one of the witnesses for a different murder case.

* * * *

At six on the dot, he knocked on Cassandra's door. He heard a bark come from inside the house. Nevan stared at the bottle of wine in his hand and frowned.

Maybe bringing wine wasn't a good idea. What if she didn't drink? Or what if she didn't like merlot?

Silently slapping himself in the forehead, he realized he was over-thinking. If Cassandra didn't like wine or merlot, she'd tell him and they could drink water for all he cared.

The dog barked again, and he heard her admonish him. "Kaiser, be quiet."

When she opened the door, he smiled. "Hello, Ms Harmen."

"You might as well call me Cassandra, Detective Largent. Please come in." She stepped back then motioned him in.

Her Seeing Eye dog sat just inside the foyer, eyeing him suspiciously. He wasn't wearing a harness, which would usually mean he wasn't working, but Nevan didn't want to assume.

"I've never seen a Rhodesian Ridgeback as a Seeing Eye dog."

Her movements were confident as she strolled across the foyer to where the dog sat. Resting her hand on his head, Cassandra nodded. "I know, but Kaiser is a one in a million dog and he was a perfect fit for me when I was looking for a new guide."

"May I pet him?" He approached but not too close. Kaiser might have been an unlikely guide dog, but he was a good guard and protective of a mistress who couldn't see.

"Certainly. Give me your hand." She held out hers.

He studied her elegant fingers before he entwined his with hers. Cassandra brought him up to Kaiser then kept him still while the dog sniffed him. Nevan glanced over at Cassandra to see her staring at him.

Bright hazel eyes seemed to be looking as deep into his soul as she could get, yet he knew she couldn't see anything. Kaiser licked his hand and she let him go.

"You see spirits all over the place, Nevan?" She took the wine he held before turning to walk down the hallway toward what he assumed was the kitchen.

"Yes." He didn't want to talk about his gift, but he knew if she were going to give him information, there would be an exchange. "I guess I was always able to see them."

Nodding, she gestured in the direction of the stool by the island. After sitting, he watched as she opened the bottle then poured some into two glasses. While she kept one, she handed one to him. The way she finished cutting up vegetables before tossing them on a cookie sheet impressed him.

"When did you lose your eyesight?" He took a sip, tasting the merlot and deciding it was passable. Of course, what else did he expect from a ten dollar bottle of wine.

Her light brown curly hair came right to her shoulders, but she had it caught up in a ponytail. The faded jeans she wore hugged her hips and ass in such a way that he couldn't help but stare at them. She wasn't skinny or even slender in the way present day media said women should be—Cassandra carried an extra pound or two, but it looked good on her.

Nevan enjoyed watching her move around the kitchen and it was obvious she'd lived there long enough to get very familiar with the place. She set the timer on the oven before joining him at the island.

"In the seventeen hundreds, I was involved in a carriage accident in England. It was a head injury, but I survived except for my eyesight." Cassandra touched her temple where he saw a small white scar.

"I believed fallen could recover from anything short of a killing wound, even during less-modern times." Nevan started to put his hand on her arm then stopped. Touching her without warning would upset her, and he wasn't interested in that.

She covered his hand with hers like she knew what he had been about to do. "I assumed that as well, but it seems God still had some secrets he wasn't willing to tell us, or he had his own reasons for me being blind."

Tilting his head, Nevan stared at her. "Do you seriously believe God chose to keep you blind instead of letting you heal like normal?"

Cassandra shrugged. "It's the one thing that makes sense to me, but I've had three hundred years to get used to the idea. I had to learn how to deal with losing my eyesight. It was hard at first."

"I bet it was," Nevan agreed.

"May I touch your face?"

Her question surprised him and he nodded.

"If you're nodding, I can't see you," she reminded him.

Chuckling, he lifted her hand to his cheek. "Go ahead. Can you see anything with your powers?"

He shut his eyes as she ghosted her fingers over his face, knowing she was learning what he looked like the best way she could.

"Aside from the visions I get, I sense emotions and presences. I can read thoughts like most fallen, but that's one thing I try not to do." Cassandra dropped her hands to the counter. She took a sip of wine before asking, "What made you decide to become a cop?"

"Hmm...I wanted to help people and I don't like fire, so I figured being a cop would be a great way to do it, plus my father and grandfather were. It's a family tradition."

"Much like what I do is a family tradition. In a way." Smiling, she stood as the timer went off.

"Can I help? And just so you know, I'm offering because my mother raised me to be a gentleman, not because I think you can't do it yourself."

"You can pour us both some more wine then set the table for me. Once I dish out the food, I'll let Kaiser outside to run around for a little bit while we eat." She pointed to the cupboard and the drawer.

Nevan did as Cassandra asked him. Eventually, they sat at her table in the dining room. He watched while she ate, so delicate and careful. She didn't drop any food or spill any wine the entire time.

"What do you want to know, Nevan? You don't have a problem with me calling you by your first name, do you?" She leaned back in her chair while focusing in the general direction of his face.

"My cousin was into the occult and very interested in our ancestry." He grimaced.

She narrowed her eyes. "And why was he so interested?"

Shrugging, Nevan tapped his fingers on the table. "Our family legends say that we're descended from some Druid high priestess. She was supposed to have had some kind of magical powers. I think if it is true, then she must have had the sight like me."

Cassandra grinned. "You found out that I'm an expert on druids and Irish history."

"Yes. Danielle Weston got me your name."

"Danielle is a fallen in Chicago, I believe," she murmured. "Why would she give you my name?"

He stood then touched her shoulder. "Why don't we clear off the table then move this conversation to the living room? It'd be more comfortable."

She didn't stiffen at his touch, so he took it as a good sign.

"Good idea. You start clearing while I go let Kaiser in."

When she rose to her feet, Nevan found himself standing entirely too close to her for his piece of mind. She glanced up at him and licked her lips. All the reasons it was a bad idea fled his mind as he bent to kiss her.

Cassandra pressed her hand to his chest, but she didn't push him away. She simply remained where she was and let it continue. Nevan ran his tongue along the seam of her mouth while encircling her waist to pull her against him. She fit into the angles of his body like she'd been made for him.

Utterly ridiculous thought, since Cassandra has been around since the world began. Yet knowing just how old she was didn't make a difference to his cock, which seemed to have taken over his mind. He slid one of his hands down to cup her ass and the other up to cradle the back of her neck.

She capitulated to his demands and opened, allowing him to sweep his tongue in. He enjoyed the taste of the wine in her mouth, wishing he could drink it from there. Her unique flavor mixed with the heady bouquet of the merlot to create something he wanted to sip every day.

A bark from outside caused her to jerk away. He kept a hold of her, not wanting her to fall or run into anything. Another bark and she moved away from him toward the back door.

"Something's wrong. Kaiser doesn't bark unless someone's here," she informed him.

For some reason, the image of the hooded man standing in his yard flashed through his mind and Nevan tensed. He reached Cassandra before she got the door open.

"Let me go out there."

He took a second to be surprised that she didn't protest, yet maybe because Kaiser didn't sound like he was hurt or in pain, it was better for him to go. She might be a fallen angel, but she was still vulnerable simply by way of her blindness.

Taking out his gun as he stepped out on the patio, Nevan searched for the dog in the waning light. Kaiser stood, hackles up and growling, in front of a large tree. As he approached, a soft whistle came from behind him, and Kaiser trotted to where Cassandra waited in the doorway.

Even before he got there, Nevan knew whoever — or whatever — it was Kaiser had cornered was gone. He went around the whole yard, checking the fence and looking for footprints. There weren't any, and a hint of unease made its way into his mind. *Could this have anything to do with last night?* He didn't know, but he was going to warn Cassandra.

Whether she was in danger or not, he didn't care. She needed to know there might be something else going on besides there being a possible killer out there. Cassandra needed to be prepared in case this became something they weren't expecting.

Once he'd returned to the house, he entered then locked the door behind him. He went to the living room where he found Cassandra curled up on the couch with Kaiser sitting on the floor next to her.

"There wasn't anyone there and I didn't see any prints anywhere," he announced.

Cassandra nodded before sipping from her coffee mug. "There's a cup on the table there. I didn't know if you took it with anything."

"Black is fine." He settled at the other end of the furniture, picking up his mug after he was seated.

"There was something out there. Like I said, Kaiser doesn't bark at nothing, plus I sensed a strange presence."

"Is that why you didn't come out with me?" Nevan eased back against the cushions, relaxing slightly. He inhaled the fragrant aroma of the hot liquid. God, how he loved the smell of coffee.

She nodded. "I can sense things and get a general idea of where things are, but I'm not very helpful in a fight or anything like that. It took me a long time to come to terms with my limitations."

"That's understandable." He set his cup back down. "Can I hold your hand?"

Cassandra held out her hand and he entwined their fingers. Again, he couldn't help thinking how perfect it felt to hold her like that, though he admitted silently that he wanted to wrap her naked body in his arms while he made love to her. Shaking his head, he knew what he wanted wasn't important at the moment.

"Last night, I couldn't sleep. It happens quite often, especially when I'm in a new place. The spirits are trying to get used to having someone around who can see and hear them. It's like a jumble of noise in my head." He tapped his temple with her fingers. "They invade my dreams and it ends up being easier just not to close my eyes."

After putting her mug down, she cupped his face with both her hands. He rested his forehead against hers and breathed in her air.

"Maybe you need to rest somewhere there aren't any ghosts," she murmured.

When she said that, he realized what had been playing around in the back of his mind. No spirits vied for his attention and none had since he'd first approached her house.

"How is that possible? All the fallen I've run into are haunted by hundreds of souls. People they've hated and loved during the centuries."

Cassandra had to have known what he was asking because she said, "I deal with my own memories and ghosts. Being blind gives me a lot of time to think and listen. I'm not distracted by the visual world around me."

"And your house? It's not new. How did you manage to clean it?" He slid his arm around her waist, drawing her closer to him.

Laughing softly, she snuggled into his side. "I had it built when I first moved out here and over the decades, I've modernized it. I cleansed the land before I let them begin to set the foundation."

Nuzzling along her hairline to her ear, he absorbed the subtle feeling of safety seeming to emanate from her. Nevan had never had the need to feel safe before, but she'd created an atmosphere where he wasn't constantly trying to block out the wraiths and spirits dogging his every step.

"It's quiet in here," he whispered against her ear.

She shivered and he couldn't help but smile at her reaction. He took her lobe between his teeth then tugged. Cassandra gripped his shoulders with her hands.

"I don't think this is a good idea," she said.

"You're probably right," he admitted, yet it didn't keep him from sucking on the sensitive flesh right behind her ear.

Letting her head fall to the side, she gave him silent permission to continue even while she said, "No, I mean it, Nevan. What do we know about each other except I'm a fallen angel and you're a seer?"

With a mental sigh, he eased away from her. As much as her body might be saying she wanted it, her mouth was saying she didn't and he wasn't going to push it further. That didn't mean he was going to let her go. He kept her in his embrace while he tried to get his mind back on whatever they'd been talking about before.

"Right. Anyway, since I couldn't sleep last night, I went to get a glass of milk. While I stood in my kitchen, looking out my back window, I saw a hooded figure standing there in my yard."

Cassandra didn't stiffen, but he could tell she had all of her attention on him.

"After getting my gun, I went out to look around. Of course, he was gone by then and to be totally honest, I can't be sure he was there physically anyway. He might have been a spirit. I just know he was there."

"Of course he was." She patted his hand. "You have to remember you're not talking to a mortal, Nevan. I know all about what exists in the world that most people can't see or aren't willing to acknowledge are real."

"Right." He did need to remember that, because it might be her knowledge that helped him solve the problem of his cousin. "I wanted to let you know about what I saw, just in case whatever it was is connected to my case."

Cassandra kissed his cheek. "Thank you for the warning."

"It's the least I can do. I wasn't very nice to Danielle before I left Chicago. She'd never treated me with anything except respect and I was a complete ass to her." Nevan chuckled. "Though in my defense, I was inundated by fallen and Lucifer made an appearance as well. Not something a man like me wants to get involved in."

Tension touched her shoulders at the mention of Lucifer.

"You met Lucifer? What did you think of him?"

It was a question he'd never been asked before. All of the Enforcers had been more worried in protecting him from the fallen angel, they hadn't been interested in what his impressions of Lucifer were. He went back to his memories of that night and shuddered.

"Lucifer is horrifyingly beautiful and tragically triumphal. He professed to disdain, yet I saw worry in his eyes for me that I'm sure the others missed," Nevan muttered as he gave voice to what he'd thought in those moments he'd been curled up in the corner of the lab at the Field Museum.

Cassandra relaxed into his arms again, and he wondered what he'd said that made her react that way. Then she shot him a questioning look. "You were involved with the Peruvian angel?"

"Yes. There were a few deaths that weren't part of the whole skeleton thing. Those dead had to do with a jewelry heist down in Peru and the thieves used Dr Carson's shipments to get them across the border." He resisted adding anything else. It was over and done with, and all he wanted to do was move on. "Do all fallen angels know each other?"

"Meaning do we have like a special connection or something?"

He nodded, brushing her hair with his chin.

"Are you nodding?"

"Yes. Sorry."

Another pat to his hand. "No problem. It's just something you'll have to get used to if you hang out with me."

He tugged her until she curled up on his lap and wrapped her arms around his neck.

Why does it feel like we've been doing this forever? I've never got so attached so fast to a woman, and I never imagined it'd be a fallen.

"We can talk to each other mentally if we choose to, but most of us tend to stay isolated. Even Enforcers prefer not to gather together. Though there will be a higher concentration of us in bigger cities." Cassandra stroked his chest while she talked and he wondered if she realized what she was doing. "To be honest, most of them stay away from me. It's like they're worried my blindness is catching and they'll get it from prolonged exposure to me."

"That's silly." Then he paused before continuing, "Of course mortals do that to those with disabilities as well, so I guess fallens aren't the only silly ones."

She laughed. "Anyway, the biggest and closest link we have is Mika'il. The archangel knows where each of us is located throughout the world. He can find any one of us with a simple thought."

Nevan swallowed. He'd run into Mika'il and just the idea of those silver eyes looking into his soul again made him break into a cold sweat. He'd rather face Lucifer a thousand times than spend one more minute with Mika'il.

"Lucifer might be able to do that as well, but I don't think he can be bothered keeping track of us. He has his mind on other things."

"Like taking over earth for his own purposes," Nevan quipped.

Cassandra shook her head. "No. God already gave him dominion over earth, why would he continue to torment mortals? He's truly not interested in taking souls or gathering more power. I think he wants to be left alone."

Nevan wasn't sure Cassandra was talking about the same Lucifer. Not after what Danielle had told him about Lucifer taking Christian's soul, but he wasn't going to tell Cassandra about that. If she didn't know about it, then she didn't need to.

"Are you friends with Lucifer?"

"I wouldn't call us friends, but he does come and visit me from time to time." She slid her fingers between the buttons of his shirt to tease the hair on his chest. "Maybe it's because I'm one of the few who doesn't blame him for my fall."

He frowned. "Why not? Seems he's the one who suggested it and led the way."

She twisted a few strands and he sucked in a sharp breath.

"He might have suggested it, but I didn't have to go along with him. I could've stood with Mika'il on the other side."

"Why didn't you?"

Chapter Three

Why didn't you?

Nevan's question echoed through her head. Why hadn't she been one of the smart ones and stuck with the *status quo*? What had convinced her Lucifer was right about the rebellion?

She shrugged. "I've gone over it through the millennium and haven't come up with one good answer. I did it, and it was my choice, so I can't lay blame on his shoulders when he doesn't deserve it."

"And that is why I come to visit you from time to time. I'm not hounded by 'it's all your fault'. Christ knows I'm tired of listening to people not taking responsibility for their own actions." Lucifer's voice danced through her head.

Cassandra heaved a sigh. *"Can we not do this tonight? I don't want to reopen old wounds."*

"You might have wounds that have scabbed over, Cassandra. My wounds are reopened every day and will never heal until the end comes."

"You're so dramatic, Lucifer. Now get out of my head."

A soft laugh and a gentle touch spoke of his leaving, and Cassandra blinked back the tears from her eyes. It wouldn't pay to have Nevan notice them and ask her what was wrong. No one seemed to understand how she could cry for the most infamous fallen angel in the world.

Nevan caressed her shoulder and she savored the heat coming from his touch soaking through her T-shirt. She let her head rest on his shoulder while working the buttons of his shirt through their holes.

"Danielle knows I'm an expert on druids and pre-Christianity Irish history, but she doesn't realize I'm a fallen. We never met face to face. I consulted on some *objets d'art* for her and we communicated through email." Cassandra peeled his shirt open then rubbed her cheek against the thick carpet of hair she could feel covering his chest.

"Umm...Cassandra," Nevan said.

"Yes?" She nuzzled the flat nipple peeking out.

"Didn't you say earlier that we shouldn't do this?" He gripped her shoulders, but didn't move her away from him.

She thought about it then licked the hardened pebble of flesh. "Yes, but I've changed my mind."

"Far be it from me to turn down an offer like this, but are you sure? I don't want you to think you should do this or anything."

Frowning, she asked, "Why would I feel like I should do this?"

Nevan cleared his throat. "Maybe out of pity or something because I told you I don't sleep well and that I feel comfortable here. It might make your feel like taking care of me."

"Oh dear." Cassandra started giggling and soon she was laughing so hard, she had to prop herself up using his body.

He kept silent, but she could feel his annoyance building and she took a deep breath to get her mirth under control. When she could talk without laughing, she cradled his face and brought his lips to within inches of hers.

"I want to have sex with you because I find you shockingly attractive. It's also an amazing turn-on to be able to be with someone who knows all your faults, yet fully accepts them and you."

Bringing their mouths together, she kissed him with all the passion she had in her. What she said was the truth. For the first time since she'd fallen, she would be sleeping with someone who knew everything about her. Well, all the important things anyway.

The moment he demanded that she open her mouth, she did so. Nevan swept his tongue in and she sucked on it. He grunted as he shifted her until she straddled his thick thighs. She'd known he was taller than her by the height of his voice when he'd stood next to her. Also, his shoulders were broad and she could feel the definition of his muscles in his chest and stomach.

She'd noticed when he'd first arrived at her house, he'd had walls built around his emotions, which she understood completely. When he could see spirits and get mobbed by them, he had to find a way to keep them out of his soul. Yet her touch seemed to be removing those walls brick by brick.

Cassandra couldn't stop running her hands over his crisp, rough hair, exploring from nipple to nipple then down to where a thin line trailed under his pants. She broke their kiss when she scooted back to fumble with his belt buckle.

"Cassandra." He stopped her with just her name.

She looked up as his gaze caressed every inch of her face. "Yes?"

"Can we find your bed? I'm not interested in our first time being on your couch with Kaiser staring at us."

Putting her hand down to the side, she grinned when Kaiser stuck his wet nose in her palm. "I guess we can. First we need to make sure everything's cleaned up down here and locked."

"Is that something you do every night?" Nevan gripped her hips then lifted her off his lap to set her feet on the floor.

"Yes. I like to have a routine and putting everything away at night before I go to bed helps. That way when I come down in the morning, I don't have to worry about a knife in the sink or something like that."

She listened as he stood and with his help, putting everything back in place didn't take long at all. They rinsed the plates then put them in the dishwasher while Kaiser went out one last time. She gestured toward the stairs.

"My bedroom is at the end of the hall upstairs," Cassandra explained.

"Go on up and get ready for bed. I'll check the doors and windows down here."

He brushed a kiss over the top of her head before tapping her on the ass to get her moving. She laughed as she headed to the bathroom. It was strange to have someone else in the house with her again.

She'd been married three times since civilization started appearing. Each husband had been lost to old age and the fragility of humans. Her heart had broken when she buried them, yet she'd never planned to keep from loving again.

Love was a natural condition of angels and mortals alike. To be so understood that someone wanted to cleave his life to hers was the ultimate goal for everyone, and Cassandra was no different.

Not that she loved Nevan. Not yet anyway, and maybe they would never grow that serious about each other, but they already had a deeper connection than she'd had with any of her other partners. Their union would be far more intimate and while knowing that scared her, she wasn't going to pass up the opportunity.

After washing up and brushing her teeth, she went to her bedroom where she stripped before climbing under the covers. She wasn't worried about condoms, though Nevan might want to use them. If he did, she hoped he had one. Not having a love life tended to insure she wasn't prepared when a man spent the night.

God had never seen fit to grace her with children with her other marriages, so she assumed fallen couldn't have offspring. When she'd first had that thought, she'd been disappointed because all she'd wanted to do was give her husbands children. Then she'd told her last husband and he'd married her anyway, saying children weren't important enough to not having the woman he loved in his life.

A few minutes later, Nevan knocked on the door and she listened to him enter. "Everything is locked up tight."

The mattress dipped where he sat. She rolled up against his back then ran her hand over it. There was a bump by his shoulder blade and one on his lower back.

"Bullet scars?"

He grunted then two soft thuds told her he'd removed his shoes. The bed returned to normal before another lighter bump said his pants were on the floor.

She scooted over when the sheets lifted a little. After encircling her waist, he shifted so that she was under him.

"Do you have a condom?"

Nevan froze. "Yeeaah." He stretched the word out.

"Did you want to use one?" She ran her hand through his short cropped hair. "I can't get pregnant, but you only have my word on it. Plus I don't have any diseases."

His heat left her for a moment then rustling came from where he'd put his pants. When he returned, a cool object dropped onto her chest. Cassandra closed her fingers around the foil square. Smiling, she set it up by her pillow before grabbing Nevan's ears to tug him up to her face.

She crushed their lips together and every inch of her body exploded with need. Entangling her arms and legs with his, she rubbed against him, loving the way his body hair scratched over her breasts.

He trailed kisses over her throat down to her nipples where he licked one then the other until she squirmed under the rather harsh texture of his tongue on her tender flesh.

"Oh." She arched when he slipped his fingers between her thighs to rub over her clit. His calluses were amazing and each press of them caused little shocks to race through her body.

Once her breasts were aching, he eased down to wedge his shoulders between her legs. The bristles on his jaws scraped the inside of her thighs then against the soft inner lips of her pussy.

"Christ!"

Nevan used his tongue and fingers to pleasure her until she could barely contain her orgasm. He took her to the edge again and again, backing off just before she went over. Just when she couldn't take it anymore, he buried four of his fingers inside her while sucking her clit hard.

Cassandra screamed as she came, tugging on Nevan's hair enough to make him grunt. When she could finally breathe, she went limp and listened as he opened the packet to roll it over his cock.

"Please, Nevan," she begged, wanting to feel him inside her. She held out her arms to him and sighed as he covered her.

After he slid in, Cassandra lifted her hips and he braced his hands on either side of her head. His breathing sped up while he thrust in and out. The cooling sensation of his sweat dripping onto her face was evidence of how hard he was working. The musky scent of sex filled the air.

His movements became jerkier and his breathing stuttered as Nevan's climax overwhelmed him. He took her harder and deeper, not that Cassandra would complain. She wouldn't mind the bruises or the ache tomorrow to have such joy tonight.

"Jesus!" Nevan surged into her then froze.

Her second orgasm of the night was smaller and shorter, but still amazing. Nevan's strength must have given out because he collapsed, yet he was polite enough to roll to the side so he didn't squish her.

She winced when he slid out of her. "Wow. That was..." She couldn't think of any words to describe it.

"Yeah." Nevan kissed her hard before climbing off the bed. Cassandra wasn't prepared when he picked her up and slung her over his shoulder. "Let's take a shower."

"Okay."

Their shower was quick then once they were dried off, Nevan carried her back to bed. This time he didn't cart her around like a bag of potatoes. He was a gentleman, making sure she was tucked in nice and tight before he started to get dressed.

"Wait. You're not staying?"

When he paused in the midst of pulling on his pants, the weight of his gaze landed on her and she smiled, hoping she looked convincing.

"Are you sure? I know you didn't plan on me being here."

"Well I'm not going to kick you out. It's been a while since anyone's shared my bed. I'd like to wake up with you tomorrow."

There was nothing wrong with being honest. The sibilant whistle of his pants sliding through his hands to hit the floor gave her a warning before he joined her in bed. He spooned her and she tangled their fingers together.

The hushed tone of Nevan's breath filling his lungs then him exhaling soothed her. Cassandra closed her eyes, focusing all of her other senses on Nevan's presence.

* * * *

Cassandra murmured and Nevan awoke as her voice grew louder. They'd moved apart during the night so she lay on her right side facing away from him. He reached out to touch her shoulder.

"Cassandra, wake up." He shook her a little, hoping she didn't startle. "You're having a dream."

She rolled on her back with her eyes wide open, yet he wasn't sure she was awake. "Don't do it."

"Don't do what?"

Frowning, she tilted her head and her voice went deeper. "The one way I can find out about the magic is if I cast a spell."

"A spell?" *What the hell is she talking about?* "Magic?"

"Aye. My bloodline descends from a powerful high priestess. I should have the sight or magic in my blood. I need to open the gate."

Nevan realized there was something different about her face. He wanted to reach over and turn the light on, but he was afraid it would wake her and he'd lose whatever was going on with her. Her face looked odd, almost like another person lived inside her.

"Gate? What kind of gate?" He shifted the pillows around so he had something to lean on while he talked to her, though he had a feeling he was chatting with his cousin.

"He says we can open a gate to welcome her back. It's time for her to return, and when she does, the power will flow." Cassandra closed her eyes and breathed deep.

Nevan wished he had a notepad and a pen to write it down because he wasn't sure if she would remember it when the dream—or vision—was over. "Who is she?"

Cassandra frowned and her voice began to sound more like her own instead of deeper. She twisted her head from side to side like she was trying to clear her mind. Nevan didn't like her being caught up in the vision, but she was telling him things he needed to know about what might have happened to Patrick.

"Come on, Patrick. Stay with me. Who is she?" He leaned over Cassandra, staring into her hazel eyes. It was obvious there was another spirit struggling with hers for her body.

"She's our ancestor, Nevan. Be careful," Patrick warned before his spirit was shoved out by Cassandra's much stronger one.

Gasping, Cassandra shot up and Nevan had to get out of the way before she nailed him in the chin. He took her in his arms, holding her tight so she wasn't alone. He smoothed his hand up and down her back.

"It's all right. I'm here and I won't let anything hurt you," he murmured in her ear.

Her unladylike snort surprised him, causing him to ease her away to look down into her face. Not that he could tell much by her blank eyes and the exhausted expression she wore.

"You do realize that I'm pretty indestructible, even while being blind." She smiled.

"Maybe you are, but you are vulnerable in many ways." Nevan pecked her cheek. "What were you dreaming of?"

"It was a vision." Cassandra snuggled back into his embrace.

He settled against the pillows then adjusted the blankets to cover them both. "Then what was the vision? I think I was talking to my cousin Patrick."

Pursing her lips, Cassandra seemed to be thinking for a moment before she said, "It's entirely possible. I was in some kind of chamber and there were twelve hooded figures circling a stone altar where another hooded figure. A man I think, but I'm not sure. I'm going off of Patrick's memories."

"You kept saying things like casting a spell, opening a gate. They want to bring a high priestess back somehow. She's supposed to be an ancestor of ours."

She shot him an amused glance. "How impressive. Descended from royalty."

"Were druids royalty?" He was quite willing to admit he didn't know anything about druids or that part of history.

"From what anyone can tell, yes, they were like royalty. They were the most important members of Celtic society, able to move among the tribes and overrule the chiefs." Cassandra ran her hand over his stomach, tracing the dips and bumps of the muscles. "They taught all of the stories and laws."

"Did they have magic?"

Having spent all of his life seeing spirits and working with fallen angels, he wouldn't have been surprised if they did.

After pressing a kiss to the middle of his chest, she chuckled. "Of course they did. They were fallen angels and some of the most powerful beings on earth during that time."

Laughing, Nevan rolled his eyes. "I should've known, and don't tell me, you know all of this because you were one as well."

She shook her head. "Oh no. I was living in Greece at the time. I had nothing to do with what was going on in Ireland and Britain. I had a few friends who were and they told me about their secrets. It helps when you want to find a job."

"Don't you work at a woman's shelter downtown?" He tried to remember what Tommy had told him.

"I do now. At one point in time, I taught Pre-Celtic history at Berkley and did some consultant work." Cassandra yawned.

"Why don't you get some more sleep? We can talk about the rest of this in the morning." Wiggling, he got them back lying under the blankets. "I'll be here when you wake up."

"Thank you." She hugged him before laying her head on his shoulder and closed her eyes.

* * * *

Nevan's phone rang as he was washing up the last of the breakfast dishes. Cassandra walked into the kitchen when he picked his phone up off the table.

"Largent."

"Hey, it's Tommy. We got a hit off some prints found at your cousin's house. I'll text you the address and you can meet me there," Tommy told him.

Nevan grabbed his shirt from one of the chairs. "Sounds good to me. I'll be there as soon as I can." He hung up then headed to the front door.

Cassandra followed him down the hall to the foyer. She propped her hip against the hall table. "Get anything good?"

"You're a consultant for the police department, so I can tell you this. Tommy said we got prints from my cousin's. We're going to pick the person up right now." Nevan dropped his phone in his jacket pocket before grabbing her shoulders to pull her close enough for a kiss. "Once we know more about this guy, I'll call you. Maybe we can meet for dinner."

"Thanks. Be careful."

Nevan dashed down the steps of Cassandra's porch to his car. After climbing in, he started his car then checked his phone for the address. He got the directions before he took off.

He pulled up next to Tommy's car and nodded at his partner as he got out. "What do we have, Tommy?"

Tommy held out a folder. "One set of prints belongs to Mr August McCallen, who happens to be the owner of this corner pub. Brings a bit of Ireland to us rather uncouth Americans."

"Have you ever eaten or stopped for a drink at August's?" Nevan skimmed McCallen's file while Tommy talked.

"No. We don't make it out this part of town. A little more upscale than Sheldon and I like."

Nevan shook his head. "You and your husband should get out more. I mean you live in Los Angeles, for Christ's sake. There are a million different restaurants and things to do every night. But you go home and have steak every night before sitting in front of the TV watching whatever it is you watch."

Tommy grinned at him, not offended at all by what Nevan said. "We like our lives the way they are. No need to shake it up." Then Tommy eyed him. "Why do you look so wrinkled? I don't think I've ever seen you look quite so disheveled. Did you literally roll out of bed to meet me here?"

Nevan glanced down at his shirt and grimaced at the wrinkles. He hadn't had time to throw it in the dryer at Cassandra's to see if they'd come out. "I didn't stay at my place last night and I hadn't planned on spending the night elsewhere, so I wasn't prepared with another shirt. I didn't have time to go home and change."

"You're finally getting some?" Tommy slapped him on the shoulder then took the file back. "Good for you. You're a good-looking guy, though I don't know many people who go for red heads."

"Thanks a lot, Tommy. Let's go bring Mr McCallen in for questioning. Maybe we'll catch a break and he'll confess to murdering Patrick."

He heard Tommy snort as he walked away. Nevan grinned because pigs would fly before they even had their first suspect confess to a crime. It usually took a lot of time and footwork to get a confession and evidence enough to convict.

Mr McCallen was quite cooperative when Nevan asked him to come down to the station to answer a few questions. They didn't arrest him, but made sure he rode with one of them instead of driving in on his own.

* * * *

The dark haired man standing on the corner watched as Nevan escorted McCallen from the pub. He narrowed his silver eyes before turning to disappear into the crowd. It was a second later that he materialized at the shelter where Cassandra worked.

"Ms Harmen, I need to speak to you outside please," he said to Cassandra when she sensed his presence.

"All right, sir." She told the other lady working the front desk with her that she would be back in a few minutes. Once they were across the street, sitting at an outdoor table, she asked, "What is it, Mika'il? Why are you here?"

"Nevan Largent just took a man in for questioning," Mika'il informed her.

"I'm not surprised. He is a cop, you know. Arresting people is his job." She folded her arms over her chest.

"McCallen is a fallen, but not an Enforcer."

Cassandra straightened in her seat while Kaiser whined from where he lay by her side. "Is he someone I need to be worried about?"

"Not yet, but he's walking a line. He might be involved with the murder you're investigating, but he's also involved in the IRA."

Frowning, she stroked Kaiser's ears to settle him down. "What does the IRA do now that they've had their cease-fire?"

Mika'il shrugged. "I don't know and I have no real idea if Nevan's techs are good enough to dig that particular gem up."

"I'll make sure to let him know, not that he'll be able to do anything about it."

Cassandra stared at the archangel and he grimaced, wishing — not for the first time — that she had retained her eyesight. Nothing much unnerved him, but being stared at by a blind person was odd. It was like they have a blank canvas and they're building images of what people look like merely by the words they use.

"Good. Remember what I told you earlier, Cassandra. Be careful with this one. Old magic can be dangerous, especially for people like us."

She nodded and he stood, drawing their meeting to a close. "You have to get back to work and I need to go."

As Cassandra headed for the cross-walk, Mika'il called out, "Have you talked to Lucifer lately?"

She stiffened for a second before she shook her head. "Haven't heard from him in months."

Mika'il didn't reply, simply watched to make sure she got across the street and into the shelter safe before he took off. "Why would she lie to me about Lucifer?" He murmured as he made his way toward the Hollywood sign. Mika'il had a meeting with some other fallen that needed to be taken care of.

Chapter Four

Cassandra turned in a circle, sweeping the room with her powers to see if she could pick anything else up. Flashes of the symbols popped into her mind and she tried to fixate on them so she could go look them up. There was something different about them and while she couldn't place it at the moment, given time she'd be able to work out what was wrong with them.

"Why do you do this?"

Coming out of her trance, she whirled to face the doorway where Lucifer stood. She could almost picture him in her mind, leaning against the doorframe with his hands in his pocket. A rather tranquil posture for him, and knowing what she did about him, she couldn't imagine why she would put him in that particular pose.

"Do what?" She wandered in the direction of his voice. Kaiser kept pace with her, though he stood on her other side away from Lucifer. Kaiser didn't like the fallen angel and she couldn't blame him. Hurt and anger shot off Lucifer like bright Chinese fireworks to stab into her mind and soul.

When she'd first discovered she had this ability, it had been so painful to be around Lucifer. She had no way of controlling her powers and he didn't seem interested in containing his own emotions. Over the centuries though, she'd gotten better and Lucifer had dulled his rage. At least he did when he was with her.

"Help them out with these crimes?" Cinnamon and sulfur filled her nose as she approached him. "Why tire yourself out when it doesn't matter?"

He loomed over her, a dark shape with red and gold streaks running in his aura. Cassandra placed her hand on his arm and gasped as a strange current raced through her.

"What was that?"

His arm shifted under her hand like he'd shrugged. "I don't know what you're talking about."

"You have someone else's power. Did you take a fallen's soul, Lucifer? You said you'd never do that." Raising her face, she sent him an accusing glare. Well, she hoped it was accusing and a glare. She was never sure what she conveyed anymore.

"Let's go somewhere else to talk, Cassandra. Being in a room coated with blood isn't where I want to spend my time." Lucifer wrapped his arm around her shoulder and a surge of energy rippled over her.

When she had sensation again, brightness beat down on her skin and she knew they weren't in California anymore or if they were, they were out at one of the beaches. The heat didn't have the same filtered feel it did when she walked around Los Angeles in the smog.

"Where are we and did you remember to bring Kaiser with us this time?" She might have been the one person—angel and human—who would talk to Lucifer that way. She wasn't afraid of him and never had been. Lucifer sometimes forgot about the dog and left him behind. Maybe that was why Kaiser didn't like him.

"Somewhere in Tahiti. I think. And yes, your dog is right by your side, none the worse for wear." Lucifer took her hand before leading her forward seven steps. "There's a chair to your left. The seat is about four inches lower than you are."

Once she found the arm, she could judge distance and height with her fingers. After sitting, she leaned back and crossed her legs. "Why did you bring me here, Lucifer? I have things to do back at home."

He chuckled and she sighed silently as the sound combined with the crash of the waves to drift over her. There was tragedy in his laugh, but there was just the tiniest hint of hope as well, and that was what she clung to.

"I hate Los Angeles. All that hustle and bustle and pollution. I'll never understand why these mortals destroy their world like they do. It's not like they'll get another one." Lucifer cleared his throat. "But my thoughts aren't important. I wanted to warn you about this case you're working on with that detective."

"I hear you had a run-in with Nevan."

"Nevan? On first name basis already?" He leaned into her and breathed deeply. "And you smell like him as well. I'm impressed, Cassandra. I never imagined you had the good sense to grab onto a man like him."

She eased back, not liking his invasion of her personal space. Nevan was the only one she seemed able to handle being that close to her without her initiating contact. "What are you? Some kind of bloodhound? Sniffing me like that."

Lucifer rubbed his thumb over her cheek and she jerked away from him. "I don't have an interest in who you fuck, my dear, but your scent has changed. I find that very intriguing. But to be honest, I don't care who you chose to share your bed. I brought you here to warn you."

"You've already done that," she pointed out as she lifted her face to the salt-scented breeze.

"I know, but the more I look into this case, the more I'm not happy about it." The creak of the chair next to her told her that Lucifer shifted in his seat. "There is something more than just a simple murder."

There was a subtle inflection in his voice warning her that he knew more than he was saying.

"What do you know about this case? What 'more' is there?" Cassandra let her hand drop to Kaiser's head then played with his ears like she often did when she needed reassurance.

Lucifer hissed and she faced him, wondering what had happened to get that sound from him. "What's wrong?"

"Nothing." He seemed to be forcing his words through gritted teeth. "I have to go, Cassandra. I'll send you back to that horrible house, but promise me you'll be careful. I wish I could tell you more about it. Unfortunately, it seems like my hands are tied when it comes to you."

"Is Mika'il around? Is that why you're leaving?"

To say the archangel hated Lucifer was an understatement. Cassandra had been caught between them when they argued, so she knew what she was talking about.

"No. The self-righteous prig isn't anywhere near here. I simply remembered a problem I have to take care of." He laid his hand on her shoulder and another dark shot of power saturated her.

When she became aware again, she sensed she was in a room and a brief flash told her Lucifer had returned her to the crime scene.

"Kaiser?" She called. The click of toenails across a hardwood floor informed her that Kaiser was with her.

Once the dog leaned against her leg, she sighed. *"Thanks for bringing me back."*

"I wouldn't leave you stranded, my dear. I might be an ass, but I'm not interested in hurting you, or anyone for that matter."

Cassandra wasn't entirely sure about that, but she didn't feel like arguing. *"You be careful, Lucifer. Someday Mika'il will run out of patience with you."*

Lucifer snorted. *"Cassandra, he never had any patience for me. Other forces are staying his hand, but maybe they should just let him go."*

Exhaustion waved over her and she didn't know if it was hers or Lucifer's.

"Remember watch yourself, Cassandra, and keep an eye on your detective. Powers are work here that could do damage to everyone if they aren't contained."

"Thanks for the warning."

Then he was gone, leaving Cassandra confused as to why Lucifer had chosen to warn her. Usually it was Mika'il who delivered cryptic messages before disappearing. Like he had yesterday.

"Cassandra?" Nevan shouted from somewhere else in the house.

"In here," she yelled back as she moved to the middle of the room again. Crouching, she pressed her hand to the floor and opened her channels.

Blood everywhere, yet she was detecting a pattern in the splatters. So maybe it hadn't been completely random. The more she studied it, the more it began to look like there'd been a purpose to the bloodletting.

"It wasn't just a random killing here. I think you're going to find out that some of this is your cousin's blood. He was killed here, but for a definite purpose. This definitely wasn't a crime of passion." She spoke out loud when Nevan walked into the room.

"Yeah. I've been thinking about what you said the other day while you were channeling Patrick. Something about a gate and a spell." Nevan approached her then touched her shoulder. "Are you sure you should put your hand in the middle of things, so to speak?"

Laughing, Cassandra straightened. "The only time it's a problem is if the blood is fresh. I can never be sure I get it off my hands and people tend to have weird reactions when they see a person with blood on their hands."

"Everyone has blood on their hands in some way or another." Both Mika'il and Lucifer spoke in her head, saying the same thing. She blinked as she tried to adjust to both of them being there. It had never happen before. She just hoped they didn't start arguing while in her head.

"I'm sure that's true."

The forward push of his aura warned her and she was ready for the kiss he gave her. Cassandra pressed her entire body against Nevan's, letting him take her weight while they embraced. She had no doubt he could support her without trouble.

He slipped his hand in her hair, twisting his fingers in the strands to hold her still. She wasn't inclined to move, but she also knew it wasn't the right place for this. Trying to step back brought resistance from him for a second then he let her go.

"This isn't the place," she murmured, stroking her hand over his chest.

"I know and I'm sorry. It's just been a long morning already and I missed you," he admitted.

She grinned as happiness surged through her. Hearing Nevan confess to missing her brought a different kind of warmth than the sunlight in Tahiti. "We just saw each other this morning before you left for work."

He chuckled. "Yeah. I'm starting to become pathetic. Anyway, have you learned anything new? I'm not sure coming here again was a good idea."

"Now that I'm prepared for it, nothing here can hurt me, Nevan. I've done this hundreds of times, so I'll be fine." She gripped his elbow with one hand while taking a hold of Kaiser's harness with the other. "Why don't you take me out for some lunch and we'll exchange information?"

"Sounds like the best offer I've had all day." Nevan and Kaiser escorted her through the house then out to Nevan's car.

"Where is Tommy?" she asked once they were all situated in the vehicle.

Nevan pulled out into traffic as he said, "He had to meet Sheldon for some kind of appointment, so they were going to have lunch together as well. We'll regroup at the station."

"Good. I like having you to myself." She rested her hand on his knee and tried not to freak out when she heard the other cars rushing past them. Even after having centuries to get used to it, she still wasn't comfortable with putting her fate in others' hands.

It was especially bad on highways or in heavy traffic. Eli was an experienced driver and she trusted him with her life and Kaiser's, yet there were times when she'd emerge from the back of the car soaked in sweat. It wouldn't be nearly so bad if she could see what was going on around her. Her other senses had developed to help compensate for the loss of her vision, but they couldn't completely take its place.

"Tell me about McCallen. Did you know he was a member of the IRA back in Belfast before he came to the States?" She pursed her lips then qualified, "He's probably still a member. One doesn't give up that connection easily."

"How did you know that? Was there something in your visions that told you that?"

His gaze whispered over her face before leaving and she shrugged. "Do you want to know the truth or would you prefer me to just say I have my sources?"

Nevan's thigh twitched under her hand, showing his discomfort. "I know you have resources that us mere mortals don't. Keeping them secret from me doesn't work. If it's something I think Tommy and the others need to know, I'll figure out a way to tell them."

"All right. Mika'il stopped by earlier today shortly after I arrived at the shelter. He informed me about Mr McCallen's affiliations. Also, I had a visit from Lucifer before you arrived at the scene."

Tension filled the car and Kaiser growled low in his throat. Cassandra hummed to reassure him.

"Does Lucifer visit you often?" Though it sounded casual, she could hear the worry and displeasure in Nevan's question.

"Yes, quite often, which I admit seems rather weird to me. All that I've heard of about him says he chooses to stay away from all of the fallen—Enforcers and unrepentants alike. The only one he bothered with was Christian, and I think that was because they used to be like brothers before the fall. Oh, and Mika'il. He lives to torment the archangel." She shook her head.

Nevan coughed like her statement shocked him. "Is that a good idea? Can't Mika'il destroy him?"

"Maybe that's why he does it. Maybe he's looking to die and since Mika'il is the one who can do it, he pushes. He hopes that one day Mika'il will forget what God told him and not stay his hand." Cassandra wrinkled her nose. "I have no real idea why he bothers the archangel so much, and it's not my place to worry about it."

"Right." Nevan fidgeted for a second. "We interviewed McCallen, and while he didn't mention anything except wanting a lawyer, we discovered he was part of a club here in the city."

She ran through the vision she'd had of Patrick's memories. "That would make sense. If he's involved, there would be more than one person and they would have to have some reason for getting together that would look normal to other people. Do you know if Patrick was a part of the same club?"

"We haven't found a connection yet, but it has to be there somewhere. Either the group buried it or Patrick did to throw everyone off." Nevan's muscle flexed as he applied the brakes. "We're here."

"And where is here?" She knew they were in the city proper as she stepped out of the car. The sound of the traffic sort of echoed like they were in a tunnel, created by the buildings on every side, blocking them in.

"I thought we could eat at Engine Co No 28." Nevan tucked her hand in the crook of his elbow.

"Oh, I've been here before. It's good." She appreciated that he waited until she had Kaiser beside her before he started walking. That way she wasn't forced to run to keep up and Kaiser could still do his job, even with Nevan there.

Once they were seated in a quieter corner, she checked to make sure Kaiser was tucked out of the way of the serving staff and other customers. It wasn't fair to them to have to avoid stepping on her dog, plus it also kept Kaiser from being tripped over. He was usually even-keeled and didn't tend to snap at people, but there wasn't any point in testing his amiable nature.

Nevan read the menu to her and she told him what she wanted to eat. If she had forewarning about what restaurant she was eating at, she'd check the menu online, using software that would read it to her, and make her decision before she got there. It was a way to be independent and not be a burden to the other people who might be eating with her.

After the waiter had been and gone, Nevan took her hand in his and started talking, "Did you get anything new from your second visit to Patrick's?"

Nodding, she began, "There is a pattern to the blood splatter. I guess I shouldn't call it splatter then. At least the newest blood. If they are druids, or think they're druids, then they were doing a ritual with it."

"Patrick said they were trying to cast a spell to open a gate for some high priestess to return," Nevan commented. The clink of metal on metal said he was playing with the silverware. "Do you think the group sacrificed Patrick?"

She bit her lip for a second then said, "Druids were said to have performed human sacrifice to their deities. It might be possible that they felt such a ritual was needed to get this priestess back."

"I wonder if it worked," he muttered.

"I haven't noticed any change in the balance in the area. Not that it would make a difference, though I would think if she was as powerful as Patrick believed, there should have been some surge or something when she returned."

Nevan's sigh was long and drawn out. "Why couldn't it have been a straight-forward murder? Normal human murders are easy to deal with. Usually love or greed causes it. With this, we have no real idea why they did, except that they might have needed his blood to cast a spell to bring back a dead druid."

She held out her hand and waited for Nevan to take it. "Don't worry. We'll figure it out. We'll just have to see if they kill again or if it was a one-off."

His hand trembled in her grip. "I'd hate to think they might start murdering more people just to complete this spell."

Cassandra wrinkled her nose, not liking the overwhelming scent of peppermint and lavender that suddenly surrounded them. She sneezed once then again. After grabbing a napkin, she tried to contain them, but she couldn't. Finally, she pushed to her feet and Kaiser came out from under the table.

"I'm going to the bathroom. I'll be back in a few minutes."

"Are you okay?" Nevan asked.

She swiped at her runny eyes. "I'll be fine. Just need to go to the bathroom."

Nevan asked one of the waitresses to show her to the restroom. Cassandra could find her way back afterwards. She just needed to get away from the smell.

Watching Cassandra and Kaiser navigate the crowded restaurant, Nevan hoped she'd be okay.

What caused the sudden sneezing attack? It couldn't have been anything we ate since we haven't got our food yet.

Before he could sit, a small woman approached him. "Excuse me, sir."

"Yes?"

She was tiny and of indeterminate age, but she studied him, her gaze sharp, like she was searching for something. "Is your friend okay? I noticed she had a little attack there."

"Oh, she'll be fine. Just went to the bathroom." Nevan smiled. "Thank you for your concern though."

"I'm Mary St Timus." She held out her hand and he couldn't refuse, as much as he didn't want to chat.

"Nevan Largent. It's nice to meet you, Ms St Timus." He shook her hand, managing to keep from grimacing at how cold and clammy her skin was.

Ms St Timus held on longer than was polite, but Nevan didn't know how to break away without being rude. His mother had taught him to respect his elders and from what he could tell, she was elderly. A hint of peppermint drifted through the air.

"It was nice to meet you, Mr Largent. Take care of your lady." Her grip tightened to the point where Nevan winced as the bones in hands ground together.

"I will, ma'am."

He dropped to his seat when she disappeared. *What the hell was that? She had a grip like a trucker.* Their food arrived at the table just as Cassandra returned. He held her chair for her then told her where everything on the table was so she could eat with making a mess.

Not that he believed she would, but he figured it had to be helpful to know where everything was to start with.

"What happened there?" He was curious.

She shook her head, her confused expression creating a little wrinkle between her eyebrows. "I don't know. All of a sudden this cloud of peppermint and lavender surrounded me. It was like I was being bathed in the stuff. I had to get away from it. Didn't you smell it?"

He thought about the hint he'd caught while talking to Ms St Timus. "Just a little bit of peppermint. Are you okay?"

"Yes, I'm fine now. I've never been a fan of lavender and to have so much of it around me, I might end up with a headache later." She ate cautiously but gracefully and Nevan found himself watching her instead of eating.

"Nevan, am I dropping food on myself or something?" She wiped her mouth with her napkin.

"What? No. Why would you think that?" He jolted out of his trance.

"I could feel you staring at me." Cassandra ducked her head. "I was worried I was embarrassing you."

Nevan set his utensils down then took her hand in his. "I'm so sorry, Cassandra. I was caught up in thinking how beautiful you are, it never even crossed my mind that you would think that."

"I've had some dates where the guys got upset with me because I've spilled or dropped something." After taking a sip of water, she smiled. "Okay. Where were we before my sneezing attack?"

He shuffled back to pick up their discussion. "I was worrying that they might kill again to get this spell cast." Then a memory hit him. "But when you were Patrick, you said something about it being our ancestor."

"Who? The priestess they want to bring back?" Cassandra wrinkled her nose while she thought.

Nevan smiled, loving her expressions while wondering if she knew she made them. "Yes. Her."

"Hmm...do you think they told Patrick that they needed blood from a descendant to make the spell work? Maybe he didn't know they planned on killing him." Stiffening, she looked horrified. "What if they come after you?"

He chuckled. "I'm a cop. It's not like they can sneak up on me. I'm not a recluse like Patrick was."

She frowned and shook her finger at him. "Don't be arrogant. Even the best trained soldier can be injured or killed. You're not Superman—or even a fallen. You can be hurt."

Grabbing her finger, he tried to reassure her. "It'll be fine. I doubt they even know I'm around here. I didn't even know I had family here until I let my father know where I was moving."

"Your family isn't close?" she asked, seemingly distracted by the mention.

"I'm close with my parents and my siblings. Not with the rest of the family. The extended members of the Largent clan are scattered all over the world. Only my dad keeps track of everyone. We figure if there's something we need to know, he'll tell us." Nevan kissed the tip of her finger then let her go back to eating. "Do you have any close friends?"

"Some of the ladies I work with at the shelter, that's about it. I don't have any close Enforcer friends or unrepentants. I'll be honest and say the closest friend I have is probably Lucifer."

Nevan fought the need to glance over his shoulder before curling up into a ball. *Why do I react this way every time she mentions his name? I've dealt with him before and it's not like he scares me.*

He mentally rolled his eyes at himself. Hell yes, Lucifer scared the shit out of him, yet he was pretty sure the fallen wasn't interested in him at all. He probably didn't make a blip on his radar.

"I didn't know he could be friends with anyone."

She lifted one shoulder in a half-hearted shrug. "I'm not entirely sure you could classify us as friends, but we talk and he visits me. Maybe he's more like the annoying big brother who always has advice, but never takes any that you might give him."

Nevan still wasn't sure he could accept that description of Lucifer, yet he realized he didn't have to. No matter what kind of relationship Cassandra had with Lucifer, it wasn't any of Nevan's business and he didn't have the right to complain.

"Do you consider Danielle a friend?"

Do I?

He went over all the situations they'd been through while he lived in Chicago and realized that he did consider her a friend. She'd dealt with his being an asshole with aplomb and graciousness.

"Yes, I do and I should probably tell her that," he commented.

"I think you should."

They finished their lunch then went out to the car. Nevan had to get back to work, so he asked, "Where do you want me to drop you off?"

"You can take me to the shelter. I'll have Eli drive me home when I'm done."

"All right. Maybe I'll have more information when I call you tonight."

He dropped her off at the shelter before heading back to the station.

Chapter Five

"He's the one," the old woman informed her leader.

"You're absolutely sure?" The leader didn't want to fail a second time. They only had so many chances at getting the spell right and bringing his lover back. It had taken several years to discover the right bloodline then more years to cultivate the right connection to get his hands on one that was right.

And you were wrong about him. He didn't have a strong enough gift to feed the magic. He pushed the voice of doubt away. He wouldn't be wrong this time.

"Yes, sir. I touched him and felt the power inside him. Very strong and the even better news is he's learned how to control it, so he's built it up over the years." Her grin would've scared the pants off a sane man, but her leader reveled in it.

"We'll have to plan it just right. The full moon rises in four nights from now. We'll have to be outside for the spell to be at its strongest." He paced the altar room. "How are the others coming?"

"The altar will be finished by then and the others are almost finished gathering what you asked for." The woman's wrinkles deepened. "How are we going to get him into our custody? He's a police officer. It's not going to be easy to trick him."

Flapping his hand at her, he said, "We'll need to devise a plan. Keep following him and see if you can find a weakness we can exploit."

Her pale amber eyes lit up. "I think I know exactly who we can use. When I approached him today, he was having lunch with a young blind woman. She's vulnerable, even with that beast of a Seeing Eye dog. We take her then exchange his life for hers. He had the look of a man in love."

He rubbed his chin while contemplating her suggestion. "Okay. Have Seamus follow her to see where the best place to snatch her is. I must go and meditate. I must be balanced in my soul for this to work."

"Yes, sir." She inclined her head before leaving him.

After stripping, he knelt in front of the candles burning on the altar, ignoring the hard, cold stone under his knees. He let his chin drop as he closed his eyes. He breathed deep several times, seeking the quiet space in his mind where all the memories of centuries were stored.

At one time, he'd been one of the most powerful druids in Ireland and he'd ruled with his wife at his side. They'd been reincarnated a hundred times throughout the years, but this time he'd come back to the world on his own and her soul was stuck, which he couldn't allow to continue.

It was time for them to begin to fulfill their destinies. They were to rule the world again, but he needed his wife with him. Their combined power would be more than any government could bring to bear. They would take this modern world and crush it beneath their feet.

Excitement crashed through him as he imagined what they would achieve once she was free. Then a sharp pain in his chest reminded him that he had to remain balanced for any of the complicated spells to work. He had been laying down a network of already cast magic to help focus the gate spell.

Even though Patrick Largent wasn't the right descendant, there had still been power in his blood, so he'd used it to set the first two layers, but he would need this other man's blood to establish a foundation for the final step.

"It won't be long, love," he whispered, and a cold breeze ran the length of his spine, bringing a smile to his face. "I can't wait to hold you again."

He refocused and began to chant, letting the rhythm and the words draw him deeper inside his head.

* * * *

Nevan watched as Cassandra strolled toward him. In her own space, she was confident and moved so fluidly that he forgot she was blind. She climbed on the bed then crawled up his body until she straddled his hips.

He'd bought a box of condoms because he wanted to fuck her more than once a night. Of course there were other things they could do, which she was demonstrating at the moment. She licked along the length of his cock to swirl her tongue around the fleshy head.

After burying his fingers in her hair, he tugged on it hard enough to get her attention. She glared at him. "What?"

"Why don't you swing your cute little ass this way? I want to make sure you have some fun while you're sucking me."

A sexy grin crossed her face when she realized what he wanted and she quickly repositioned her body so that he was face to face with her most private part. Nevan licked his lips as he ran his fingers down between her legs to tap against her clit. She jumped and he was happy she hadn't taken him back in. He didn't want her to bite him.

"Ah," he moaned when she swallowed him down to the root. He was impressed by her ability. It wasn't like he was big or anything, just most of the women he'd been acquainted with hadn't liked giving head, and it had been like a negotiation to get a blow job from them.

Cassandra was quite enthusiastic about it, making Nevan very happy as well. He pinched her clit lightly before gathering some of her juices to ease his way inside her. Crooking his fingers, he scraped over the most sensitive spot inside her and the vibration of her groan around his erection caused him to shudder.

Three fingers later, Cassandra was impaling herself on them along with his tongue while he fucked her face. From the sounds she made, Nevan had the idea that she enjoyed everything happening to her. Her body welcomed his invasion with warmth and moisture.

When his own climax threatened to overtake him, he slapped her butt and she let him slide out of her mouth to glance at him. The desire on her face made him even more eager to fuck her.

"I want to come inside you," he said.

She blinked as she worked through what he said. Once it made sense, she started to roll over on to her back.

"No."

He maneuvered her so she was on her hands and knees while he knelt behind her. Nevan caressed her cheeks once before he tore the foil open to get the condom out. Maybe after they'd been together for a while, he'd stop using protection. It wasn't that he didn't believe her when she said she couldn't get pregnant, he just felt better using it.

Nevan bit back a groan as he rolled the latex down over his heated flesh. One or two hard pumps and he'd come. He didn't want that. Like he'd told Cassandra, he wanted to be inside her when his climax hit.

Cassandra didn't move as he took his time sinking into her, even though he could feel the fine tremors racking her body. They both sighed when he was finally seated all the way in. He wrapped his arm around her waist before sinking back on his heels and bringing her with him.

While sitting so intimately on his lap, she let her head fall back to rest on his shoulder. He stared over her shoulder at her breasts, which he cupped with one hand. Nevan bit her shoulder as he lifted her then let her drop.

"Oh God!" She cried as he filled her.

"You're so fucking beautiful," he whispered in Cassandra's ear as he twisted her nipple with his finger and thumb.

"Nevan." The breathless quality of her voice told him how close she was to the pinnacle.

After encouraging her to brace her hands against the wall at the head of the bed, he gripped her hips tight enough to leave bruises. He slid almost all the way out then slammed back in.

She screamed as he continued to drive into her. He watched the muscles in her back flexing with each thrust in, and two jagged scars on her shoulder blades caught his attention. He managed to peel one of his hands away from her before reaching up to trace each scar.

Forming any kind of question was impossible so he filed it away to ask at a later time. His balls drew close to his body and his cock swelled even more. It felt like he was going to explode into a million pieces at any moment and he didn't want to shatter alone.

Nevan slid his hand down though the nest of curls covering her pussy and pressed his thumb hard against her clit. He kept up the unrelenting stimulation, wanting her to come first. Finally, her inner muscles clenched like a clamp around his shaft as her orgasm hit her. He rode her through it until he couldn't control it any longer and he let go. The shockwave of his climax echoed through his entire body as he spilled his cum inside the condom.

Her residual trembling massaged him until he was sure every last drop drained from him. Cassandra went limp in his arms and he kissed the nape of her neck as he lowered them onto the bed. Lying on his side, he spooned with her until his breathing calmed. Once he was sure he could move without crumbling to a puddle beside the bed, he climbed out to head to the bathroom.

Nevan dealt with the condom then washed. Bringing a cloth back with him, he set about cleaning her up, even if only to get rid of some of the sweat that coated her tanned skin. He tossed the cloth in the direction of her laundry basket before rejoining her in bed.

Pulling the covers up around them, he brushed her hair off her forehead. "Are you okay? I wasn't too rough or anything?"

She shook her head. "Oh no. You were fine. I'm fine. Just pleasantly tired."

As silence filled the room, he listened to the click of toenails on the floor as Kaiser wandered into the room. The dog slept beside Cassandra's bed and wouldn't come into the room until they were done making love.

With all of them together, Nevan relaxed, letting his worries about the case and the possibility that he might be a target go. He wanted to get a good night's sleep and even with the extra activity he and Cassandra engaged in for the last three days, he'd gotten more rest at her house than he had at any other place he'd ever lived in.

"It's been five days since you found out that your cousin was missing. Not much has seemed to happen." Her voice was low.

"I know, but we'll catch a break in the case soon. I have faith, plus we're still working the McCallen angle. I'm sure there's something there. It just hasn't popped into my brain yet."

Cassandra patted his hand where it lay on her stomach. "It'll come to you."

"I wish we'd find his body though. My aunt wants to have something to bury. She wants a gravesite to visit." He'd received a call from his father earlier that day telling him that exact same thing.

"It'll turn up," she said. "I don't think they did anything to destroy it. They were interested in Patrick's blood. He didn't have the sight, did he?"

Nevan shook his head. "No. As far as I know, I'm the only one in my generation that has it."

"You were blessed."

Snorting, he couldn't keep his disbelief from shining through. "Blessed? I don't call seeing spirits a blessing. It's been a curse most of my life."

Cassandra changed positions so she faced him. *Why does she do that when she can't see me?* She placed her palm on his cheek. "You've chosen to look at it as a curse, but if you used it as a gift, you wouldn't be so haunted by it."

"Haunted? Was that a joke?" He laughed then cringed at the bitterness in it. "The second night I spent here was the first full night's sleep I've had in my life. It's hard to close your eyes when you know what's standing over the bed watching you."

"You've never wanted to see if you could help those spirits who appeared to you?"

"Why would I? There's nothing I could do about them. It's not like I'm a priest or a fallen angel who could send them to where they needed to go."

She smiled. "No you aren't, but what you are is a policeman. Most of those you see died violent deaths and are asking you to help them find justice. If you listen, you can hear them as well as see, then you might be able to discover who killed them."

He'd never thought about his ability as anything but a burden. *What if she's right? What if I can help them in some way? It might be worth seeing them all the time to get a chance to bring them peace.*

"Why don't you think about it? We don't have to do anything about it right now. You have other things to focus on." She kissed him then rolled back to her original spot.

Nevan wanted to whine about her giving him all of this to think about then rolling over to go to sleep. How was he supposed to rest now? Closing his eyes, he took a deep breath, held it for a few seconds then let it out, hoping it would relax him.

Then, just when he'd gotten a handle of everything and was about to doze off, his phone rang. "Son of a bitch," he muttered as he grabbed it off the nightstand.

He swore he heard Cassandra giggle as he answered, "Largent."

"They found a body," Tommy announced.

"Do we have an ID yet?" Nevan slid out of bed before pulling on his jeans.

Tommy whistled—to get someone's attention, Nevan assumed—but he held the phone away from his ear. He returned it when he heard Tommy's voice. "Not yet, but something tells me it's your cousin."

He paused in the process of putting on his shirt. "What makes you say that?"

"The fact that he's pretty much drained of blood. Not sure how they did it, but of course, there was quite a bit at his house." Tommy sounded like he was trying to figure the logistics out, but Nevan didn't care.

"I can have my aunt send some dental records out if we need them." He sat on the edge of the bed to put his shoes on.

Cassandra rubbed his back and he took a moment to lean into her touch. It was nice to know he had someone who cared to come back to.

"No. You know what he looks like, right? And we have pictures of him, so that'll be fine. His face isn't bad."

"Text me the address. I'll be there as soon as I can." After hanging up, he let his hands dangle between his knees. "Tommy thinks they've found Patrick."

"I'm sorry," Cassandra whispered.

He lifted his shoulders then dropped them. "I knew it was bound to happen, and it's not like I didn't know he was already dead. I just hate having to identify him."

"Do you want me to go with you?"

"No, honey. You stay in bed. If I can, I'll come back here. If not, I'll call you in the morning." He kissed her goodbye before he left.

* * * *

Getting to the dumpsite thirty minutes later, Nevan stalked to where a group of people were gathered. He glanced over to see Tommy watching him.

"You up to this? We can just go by pictures."

He nodded. "We weren't close or anything. Let's just get it over with so the coroner can take the body."

Tommy gestured to one of the techs who unzipped one end of the body bag. Nevan studied the bloated, pale and bruised face for a minute then nodded. "That's Patrick."

"All right. You can take him to the ME now."

Nevan wandered a little way away toward the cars, knowing that he wouldn't be compromising the scene in that direction. Propping his hands on his hips, he stared up at the black sky above him. For just one second, he felt like asking God why it had had to happen. He wouldn't do that though, because he'd learned God had nothing to do with senseless tragedy any more than he had to do with the happiest occasions in the world.

It wasn't that he didn't believe in God. Oh he did because of everything he'd seen that wasn't part of the normal world. It was just that he didn't necessarily think God watched over every single second of every single person's life here on earth.

"Sorry, man." Tommy slapped him on the back. "I assume you're going to want to break the news to your aunt and family."

"Yeah, though they know he's dead. They'll be happy to know we found his body. The closure will be when they bury him."

He scrubbed his hand over his face, trying to get back into the policeman state of mind. He didn't want to miss any clues that would lead to catching who did this. Nevan turned back to look at the dumpsite.

"Have we found anything yet?"

Tommy clicked his tongue against his teeth—an annoying habit Nevan had discovered his partner had when he was thinking. "One of the uniforms found a blood stained white robe. There's no way of knowing until the labs come back, but I wouldn't doubt we find out that the stains were from Patrick."

A white robe. Nevan filed that information away. So he really did have a link to that group Cassandra had seen in her vision. It looked it was a druidic ritual gone bad or maybe not bad, considering how much they'd taken. Maybe Patrick had to die to make the magic work.

Nevan shook his head. No matter how much he believed in spirits and fallen angels, he never assumed he'd be involved in something that had to do with magic, and apparently blood magic at that.

"We're still scouring the scene." Tommy poked Nevan in the side. "Who are you seeing? Those are the same clothes you left work in yesterday."

He trusted Tommy to take a bullet for him and to back him up when he needed it, but he wasn't going to tell him about Cassandra. Not yet at least. He wanted to talk to her about it before he started telling everyone about their relationship.

"I'm not telling you yet. Too early. Don't want to jinx it."

Tommy nodded wisely. "Gotcha. I was the same way when I started seeing Sheldon. Didn't tell anyone for a year. I wanted to make sure he was the right one before I got my mom all worked up over nothing."

Nevan walked toward his car. "Do I need to stay here any longer?"

"No. I'll stick around for a little bit longer, but I'll see you in the office tomorrow."

"Thanks." He waved before he climbed into his vehicle. An uneasy feeling crawled up his spine and he just knew there was a spirit in the backseat. Gritting his teeth, he looked in the rear view mirror and shrunk back when he met Patrick's gaze. "Fuck!"

Patrick blinked then smiled when he realized Nevan could see him. He gestured wildly and Nevan nodded.

"Yeah, I can see you, but damned if I know what you're trying to say," he muttered. After turning the car on, he pulled into traffic, trying not to get too distracted by the upset ghost sitting behind him.

"Listen, Patrick. I see you. I don't know how to go about hearing you. If you can stick with me, I can take you to someone who might be able to hear you. Do you understand me?"

Patrick nodded and Nevan noticed how nice-looking his cousin was. Thank God, he didn't look like his body did. Nevan didn't think he would be able to deal with seeing that face every time he looked up.

"Did August McCallen have anything to do with this?"

His cousin nodded. Well, it wouldn't be admissible in court, but it helped Nevan to know they were on the right path.

"Was he the one who killed you?"

Patrick shook his head then said something. Nevan shrugged to show that he didn't understand.

"Does this have anything to do with a group of druids looking to open a gate to somewhere?"

If a ghost could beam with happiness, Patrick did. Nevan tried to think of other questions, but before he could, his phone rang. Using the Bluetooth, he answered, "Largent."

"Hey. I was just checking up to make sure you're okay," Cassandra said.

He smiled. "I'm fine—or as fine as I can be, considering I just ID'd my cousin's body."

"That's rough." Cassandra cleared her throat. "Were you coming back tonight?"

"I'd like to, if it's all right." He didn't want to push himself on her, but her place was neutral territory when it came to spirits.

He could hear the smile in her voice. "It's fine if you come back. I realize after you left that you don't have a key to get back in. I'll stay up until you get here."

"I'm going to bring some company." No point in surprising her by just showing up with Patrick.

"Oh okay. I have a guest room they can use. "

He chuckled. "I'm not sure he can sleep. Of course, he's already dead so it's a moot point anyway."

"Dead?" There was a second of silence then she said, "Is Patrick's spirit with you?"

Nevan glanced in the mirror to check. "Yes. He's still there."

"Well this could be interesting. We might learn some things."

"I already know that McCallen was involved, though I have no idea in what capacity. I can see him, but I can't hear him."

Cassandra sighed. "That's to be expected. You've spent all of your life walling them out that you never developed the ability to hear as well. Though I'm not a hundred percent sure those gifts always go together."

Nevan exhaled. "Good. I don't care at the moment which I have. All I want to know is, do you think you could hear him? He might be able to help us find who killed him."

"I might. Just get him here and we'll go from there." She hung up without saying goodbye.

"Goodbye to you," he mumbled as he checked the spirit's presence one more time before he concentrated on getting them both to Cassandra's.

Cassandra met him at the door when he got to her house a little later. She threw her arms around him, holding him tight. He buried his face in her hair, breathing in her floral scent.

"I love you," he announced.

She stiffened and pulled away from him. "What did you say?"

He could pretend he'd said something else. He hadn't meant to tell her that so soon. It had only been a few days and how did he know that he felt that way? Yet he looked into those gorgeous hazel eyes that didn't see actual images, but could see into the soul of a man, and he knew it was true.

"I love you," he said again.

"Are you serious?" She grabbed his hand to drag him into the living room where she dropped on the couch. He joined her.

"I wouldn't have said it if I didn't mean it." He cupped her face in his hands then lifted so he could kiss her. "I know it's probably way too soon, but we know each other, Cassandra. We know each other's deepest and darkest secret. There's nothing to hide."

She kissed him back then said, "I love you too, Nevan."

Something settled in his soul like there'd been a piece missing and now it was back. He was complete when before he'd struggled to find his place in the world.

Chapter Six

Nevan could've knocked Cassandra over with a feather. She was so shocked by his admission that she wasn't completely sure she wasn't still asleep and it was all a dream.

"I love you too, Nevan," she said.

"Good for you, Cassandra. You were always the bravest of us." Lucifer's voice traced a whisper through her mind.

"You can be brave."

"I know I can be brave," Nevan replied and she blinked.

Shit! She'd said that out loud. Cassandra kissed Nevan again before he could say anything else.

He wrapped his arms around her waist then pulled her onto his lap. She ended up straddling his thighs. She ground herself against the bulge under the zipper of his jeans. The crotch of her panties was wet, and she shuddered at the slightly rough feel of the cotton fabric over her clit.

Nevan ran his hands down her back to cup her butt then squeezed her cheeks before slipping under her clothes. He broke their kiss. "We need to get these off you."

She stood on the couch, one foot on either side of his legs. Bracing her hand on his shoulder, she let him strip off her underwear and T-shirt. After he did that, he brought her pussy to his mouth.

He ran his tongue over her inner lips then, using one hand, he spread them to expose the piece of flesh that brought her the most pleasure. Tongue, lips and teeth were applied to make her squirm and beg until need blocked every word she could think and all she could do was moan.

Then he pushed three fingers in at once, and she bowed, savoring the burn and stretch. Once she got used to it, he started alternating between them and his tongue.

"Oh Nevan," she groaned.

Her orgasm hit her and she cried out as she came. When her legs couldn't hold her any more, Nevan helped her lie on the couch. She smiled up at him, knowing he leaned over her. She heard the jingle of his belt buckle, then the hiss of his zipper as he pulled it down. The rustling sound of jeans being pushed down to the floor caught her attention next.

She held out her arms to welcome him against her. His weight pinned her to the cushions but Cassandra didn't care. She loved the heat of him and the strength of his body. It made her feel safe and cared for in a way she hadn't felt in a long time.

He eased her thighs apart then positioned the head of his cock at her entrance. "I love you," he breathed against her lips as he invaded her core.

Cassandra raised her hips, encouraging him to go as far as he could without stopping or worrying about hurting her. All she could think about was Nevan coming inside her and giving him the joy she'd felt.

They moved together in a dance to music she swore only played in their minds. It was perfect and beautiful and everything she'd been looking for. Oh, she'd loved her late husbands, but there hadn't been this link with them that she had with Nevan.

He licked down to her nipple then sucked on it in rhythm with his thrusts, and she held the back of Nevan's head to keep him there.

"Nevan, I love you."

Her declaration was all he seemed to need to lose control. His movements grew less smooth and fell apart at the end. He thrust as deep as he could, and yelled her name as he flooded her.

The heat shocked her and she realized he didn't use a condom. Again, it wasn't like she could get pregnant, but he'd seemed rather concerned about protection and she hadn't challenged him on it. It hadn't mattered, yet now he'd made love to her without a condom. And that was the surest sign of his love.

She held him as he shuddered and trembled until he collapsed in her arms, sweaty and panting. He kissed her for a few breathless minutes before he heaved himself off her. Cassandra wrinkled her nose at the feel of his cum trickling down her legs when he helped her stand.

A heavy silence filled the room and she knew it was right then that he realized what he'd done. Reaching out to put her hand on his chest over his heart, she smiled up at him.

"I don't mind. I told you I can't have children and fallen angels can't carry human STDs. So even if you have one, I can't get it."

"I don't have a STD."

She couldn't help but laugh at how insulted he sounded.

"Let's go take a bath, then we can go back to bed."

A cold breeze hit her and she froze.

"Fuck!" Nevan was shoving her arms into his shirt and covering her up. "I forgot about Patrick."

His cousin.

"Did he watch us?" Admittedly, being watched while having sex wasn't that big a deal for her. But it might upset Nevan to have anyone else see her naked, even if that person was dead.

"I don't think so. He just appeared and you walked through him."

That would account for the cold spot. She organized her thoughts. "All right. I'm going upstairs to clean up and get dressed. I'll be right back down. Don't get started until I come back."

"I'm making some coffee," Nevan muttered.

"Can you let Kaiser out?" she called as she dashed upstairs.

"Yeah."

Cassandra washed up then dressed as quickly as possible. The entire time she could hear a low murmuring in the back of her head and it wasn't Lucifer or Mika'il. Whoever it was sounded irritated and a little scared. The voice wouldn't clear until she concentrated on it, but she didn't want to do that until Nevan was there to listen.

As she came back down, Nevan yelled from the kitchen. "We're back here."

"We?" She got another face full of cold air.

"Yeah, my cousin Patrick who you just walked through again. Hey, man, she can't see you, so that's just rude." Annoyance tinted Nevan's voice.

Laughing, she took her usual seat at the table and found her coffee mug right where she always set it ready for the next morning.

"Be careful. I filled it a little fuller than usual," Nevan warned.

"Thanks." She took one cautious sip before setting her cup down and waved her hand in the general direction of Nevan. "Should we get started? I've been hearing him talking in the back of my mind since he arrived. I need him out of there or I'll get a headache."

Nevan took the seat to her right and while she had no idea where Patrick was, she sensed his presence.

"This is how it's going to work. I'll ask Patrick the question and you tell me what he's saying, Cassandra," Nevan ordered.

"Sounds good to me." Taking a breath, she cleared her mind then welcomed Patrick to come up front and center. He came in a rush, shouting and begging. "Slow down. Stop shouting."

Nevan took her hand and she squeezed it, more for his reassurance than hers. She'd done this sort of thing before. Once he realized she wasn't going to block him, he'd calm down and they could get started.

"Patrick, shut up."

Patrick went quiet in her head and she sighed. "Okay, I can hear you, so you don't have to shout. Just talk normal."

"I can't believe I'm fucking dead, man."

"I'm sorry about that," she told him.

"Well, that's what I get for wanting to gain power. They fed me all the right lines and I fell for them."

"Do you know who killed you, Patrick," Nevan asked.

"Yes and no. I don't know their names and I never saw their faces. It was a group of neo-druids, or at least that's what I thought they were."

She repeated his answer word for word.

"You thought they were?"

She almost saw him shrug. "I went to this club meeting, right? McCallen was the one who invited me. Anyway, the club isn't where these people are. I was contacted at a meeting. If I wanted to know more about ancient druids, I should go to this fountain in this park."

"Please wait for a second while I tell Nevan," she requested.

Patrick fell silent, so Cassandra quickly updated Nevan on what he'd told her.

"What fountain? What park? I need specifics, Patrick."

She gave him the directions to get there like Patrick had received them.

"So once you got there, what happened?"

There was the faintest scratch of a pen on paper. Of course, Nevan would be taking notes. None of what he got was admissible in court because no one would believe a ghost told them about it, but it could give them leads to follow.

"I stood there for ten minutes and no one came. Just as I was about to leave, someone hits me over the head and I'm out. When I wake up, I'm dressed in this white robe in the corner of this stone room. There was a circle of twelve hooded figures surrounding an altar where a thirteenth person stood. I could hear his voice, so I knew it was a guy."

This time Patrick paused on his own, obviously having figured out that Cassandra would need time to inform Nevan.

"How many times did you go to these ceremonies?"

Patrick hummed as he thought and Cassandra was annoyed by it. "I went to maybe six ceremonies and *chatted with a few of them online. If you check my computer, you'll see the emails. Anyway, I told them about our family and how we have the gift and all that."*

"Did you tell them you had the gift?"

"I might have." He sounded like a little kid. She pictured him with his hands behind his back and kicking at the ground when caught in a lie.

"Why the hell did you do that? You don't have the gift. Hell, I'm the only one who has it that I know of." She assumed Nevan was yelling in the direction of the spirit in the kitchen.

"I wanted them to like me. Then one of them said we could bring back this high priestess and that she was our ancestor. All it would take was some blood." A snort filled her head. *"I should've known that meant I would give all my blood for it."*

The interrogation went the rest of the night and into the morning until Cassandra couldn't deal with it any more. Her head ached and she was so tired. Nevan tucked her into bed after she took some aspirin.

"Stay in bed all day if you want," he told her. "I have to go to the station and talk to Tommy. Patrick gave us some good leads, but I have to make sure I proof them with solid evidence."

"Be careful, Nevan. Patrick told us what we suspected. They wanted his blood—or your family's blood—and they're not interested in taking a pint. They'll kill you if they can get a hold of you."

"I'll be fine, love. Take care and I'll call you later."

She dropped off to sleep shortly after he left.

* * * *

It was the feeling of being stared at that woke her a couple of hours later.

"Is someone there?" she asked then opened her senses.

There was a male standing at the end of the bed, and it definitely wasn't Nevan.

"Who are you?"

"They said you were blind. Shit!"

She'd startled him into talking and now that she had a true direction of where he was, she could plan out her escape. Maybe she could keep him talking. The darkness of her room never bothered her, but it might be a source of difficulty for him.

"Where is my dog?" She wondered why Kaiser hadn't barked when the man entered the house.

The intruder snorted. "Don't worry. I took care of him. He won't be making noise or trying to save you."

Anger rolled through her. "You better not have killed him. If you did, I'll kill you with my bare hands."

"Pretty vicious for a blind chick." He edged toward the right side of the bed and Cassandra eased to the left.

"I might be blind, but I'm far more dangerous than you would ever believe," she warned.

He laughed. "Right, lady. You're not very big and carrying a little extra weight. I think I can take you."

Did he just call me fat? Oh hell no. She launched herself out of the bed and toward the hall. Right into the arms of someone who had been waiting out there. *Someone's smarter than the idiot in the bedroom.*

She struggled and punched. She kicked and bit, but she couldn't get free. Having the ghost session with Nevan and Patrick must have worn her out. When it became evident that she couldn't escape right then, she stopped fighting.

No point in exhausting myself. Need to conserve energy for later. Then she remembered Lucifer. *"Lucifer, I need help."*

"If you're picking out china patterns for your wedding, Cassandra, you can count me out of that torture."

"No!"

His astonishment at her yelling at him came through. *"All right. I was joking, you know."*

"Please, Lucifer, you need to come and check on Kaiser. I'm being kidnapped and I'm afraid they hurt him."

"Kidnapped! You're taking this all rather calmly. You know you are stronger than those mortals. I'm assuming they're mortals. Maybe they're unrepentants looking to get pay back for something you did to them. What have you been doing lately, woman?"

She gritted her teeth as they dragged her down the stairs and out of the house. She shivered. It might be sunny, but she wasn't really dressed to be wandering around outside. Her bare feet hit every stone and stick in the driveway. Being dressed in panties and a T-shirt wasn't great gear to try and facilitate an escape.

"She's perfect. That guy will come running when he finds out we have her. It's almost like taking candy from a baby." One of the guys boasted as they tossed her into the back of some kind of large vehicle.

She hissed when her knees scraped over a metal floor. "You didn't have time to grab me a pair of shoes or maybe different clothes. Won't people look at me weird being dragged into some place in my nightshirt?"

"Nope. Don't have time, lady. Have to get you to the big guy, then get back to the city to get in touch with your man." It was the talker. So far the other guy hadn't said a word.

Cassandra tried to get a bead on him, but while his presence gave off a dangerous and deadly vibe, she couldn't get much more than that from him. All she did know for sure was that they were human. Neither one was a fallen.

"Thank God for small favors," she muttered as she tried to get comfortable on the cold floor.

"They aren't fallen, Lucifer. Please just go check Kaiser out. I know he doesn't like you, but you're the only one I can contact at the moment. I need to figure out where they're taking me. I think they want to exchange me for Nevan."

"The detective? Whatever for? Did he piss off some drug cartel or something and you got in the middle of it?"

"Please. Can we not discuss it right now? I'm kind of busy." She rolled her eyes.

Lucifer sighed, showing his own frustration at her dodging his questions. *"You do remember who I am, right? I could take your soul right here and now."*

"You can take it any time you stop by to talk to me. You haven't yet, so I'm thinking you're not interested in it."

Silence from his end told her she was probably right. The van she rode in turned too fast and she wasn't prepared. She flew across the empty space then her head hit the protruding wheel well. Her mind went as dark as her vision.

* * * *

Nevan frowned as he left a message on Cassandra's voicemail.

"Who were you calling?" Tommy asked as he strolled by with a sheaf of papers.

"Cassandra," Nevan said, not thinking about keeping it a secret. Something was wrong. Every instinct in his entire body was yelling and flashing bright red warning lights.

"Why would you be calling Cassandra?"

"What?" He looked up to see Tommy staring at him with a curious light in his gaze.

Tommy repeated the question. "Why would you be calling Cassandra?"

"Because we've been sleeping together for the past week and now something's wrong." After standing, Nevan grabbed his jacket. "I have to go to her house."

His partner grabbed his own jacket then followed him out to his car. His announcement had so stunned Tommy apparently that the man couldn't think of anything to say the entire ride to Cassandra's.

Pulling into Cassandra's driveway, Nevan spotted a tall blond man standing on her front porch. He slammed on the brakes, jerking both him and Tommy against the seat belts. Lucifer stared at him through the windshield.

"Fuck no! This day cannot get worse," Nevan swore as he climbed out of the vehicle. "What the fuck are you doing here?"

He struggled against all the spirits surrounding Lucifer. They rushed him and his head filled with their clamoring while lights and colors blinded his eyes. He dropped to the ground, encircling his head with his arms, trying to get them to stop.

"Enough."

The command banished all the ghosts gathered around Nevan and his head went back to normal. Peering up through his fingers, he saw Lucifer standing over him, arms across over his chest and a rather skeptical look on his face.

"You're the one Cassandra has fallen in love with? I'm not sure about her taste any more. You're not very inspiring hero material. And your partner there." Lucifer gestured to where Tommy sat, seemingly frozen in the car. "He'll not have your back in any kind of fight. Maybe you should ask for a new one."

"He does just fine against mortals, jackass. There isn't a person—or fallen for that matter—who would be able to deal with you." Nevan climbed to his feet before brushing off his clothes. "One more time. What the fuck are you doing here?"

"Cassandra asked me to check on Kaiser for her," Lucifer told him.

Nevan took a deep breath and swallowed the tears that threatened to fall from his eyes. It had been the same way the last time he'd heard the ultimate fallen angel talk. He'd told Cassandra that Lucifer was the most horrifyingly beautiful and tragically triumphal person/angel he'd ever met. Beautiful with black eyes and gorgeous Norse God looks. Horrifying because of the agony and rage roiling around in those eyes. Tragic with that cross branded into his left cheek begging to tell the story of his fall from grace. Triumphant with thrown back shoulders and a 'never bow down to anyone' attitude. Yet whenever he spoke, all Nevan could hear was broken church bells pealing for a fallen man.

What Lucifer said forced itself through the spell Lucifer had spun over him. "Cassandra asked you to check on Kaiser. Why isn't she here to look for herself? Why did she leave without him?"

Lucifer pursed his lips while studying Nevan like he was trying to find out what Cassandra saw in him. Finally, he shrugged. "Seems she's been kidnapped."

"Kidnapped?" Nevan started to reach out to grab the front of Lucifer's shirt then stopped just short when the fallen raised one eyebrow, daring him to touch him. "Why the hell didn't you call me when she told you about it?"

"To be honest, the thought never crossed my mind. You're human, for all that you have this gift." Lucifer waved his hand vaguely toward the ghosts gathering at the very edge of the lawn. "I rarely think about mortals, and the few seconds I do, it's more about how you're annoying me."

"She could be seriously injured or dead, for Christ's sake."

Lucifer winced, but shook his head. "She's not dead, though I think she got knocked out somehow."

Nevan wanted to take him and shake him as hard as he could, then throw him off the nearest cliff. Clenching his hands to keep from doing just that, he forced a smile to his face.

"She got knocked out?" He enunciated each word slowly like he was talking to someone feeble-minded.

"Yes. We were talking while they kidnapped her and she asked me to check on Kaiser, who is fine by the way. Must have been drugged or something because he's sleeping like a puppy in his bed in Cassandra's room." Lucifer pointed toward Cassandra's bedroom window.

"Wonderful. Now getting back to Cassandra."

"Right. We were chatting then she went silent and I couldn't feel her in my head. Now to be honest, I can't feel most of the fallen. No matter what anyone tells you, I'm not in charge of them. Once we got kicked out of heaven, my job was done. I'm not a babysitter, you know." The corners of Lucifer's lips quirked up when Nevan growled. "It's your fault."

Nevan jerked at his accusation. "What?"

"You ask a lot of questions. You should've been a reporter instead of a cop, though cops do ask questions too. I guess you might be on the right career path after all."

The vein at his temple throbbed. "Lucifer, I'm trying very hard not to pull my gun and shoot you right now."

Lucifer must have decided to take pity on him or he'd gotten bored with it all. "Apparently whoever took her wants to trade her for you. I'm sure you'll know what she's talking about. But they're not fallen. Mere mortals, which is usually how it happens. Anyway, they took her and I think you'll probably get contacted at some point as to where the exchange will take place."

"Can't you find her?" Panic started to kick in. Cassandra was blind and while she wasn't completely helpless, her lack of vision did handicap her in some ways.

"No. I'm not a bloodhound to sniff her out. If you want someone to find her right away, you might want to see if you can get a hold of Mika'il. He seems to be able to find anyone he wants to find, whether they want it or not." Lucifer jerked like he'd been poked with a cattle prod. "I have to go. I have the utmost confidence that you and your very efficient partner there can find Cassandra."

To Nevan's complete and utter surprise, Lucifer disappeared in front of him. Whirling around, he couldn't see any sign of the fallen, and he was appalled that he'd taken off without even offering to help find Cassandra.

"Who the hell was that and where the fuck did he go?" Tommy joined him and Nevan couldn't even be angry with him for not getting out of the car sooner. It took a certain kind of crazy to face off with Lucifer.

"We can't focus on him right now. Cassandra has been taken, and I think it's by the same people who killed my cousin." Nevan dashed up to the front door and almost ran face first into it. He tried the door, finding it locked. "What the fuck? He locked the fucking door after he left?"

"You forget I don't need keys to get in places."

Yanking out his phone, Nevan glanced at Tommy before placing the call.

"Danielle Weston."

"Danielle, I need your help in a bad way."

"Certainly, Nevan. What do you need?" Danielle was a far better friend to him than he'd ever been to her.

"I need to talk to Mika'il ASAP." He inhaled, then slowly let it out. "Cassandra's been kidnapped and I don't know where she is. I'm afraid they want to trade her for me, and while I'm willing to do that, I'm not willing to wait for them to contact me."

Danielle was quiet for so long, Nevan actually checked his screen to make sure she hadn't hung up on him.

"I'll see what I can do, Nevan, but Mika'il isn't the kind of guy you demand an audience with."

"Well, seeing how Lucifer declined to help me, Mika'il is my only choice."

She inhaled sharply. "You asked Lucifer for help? How did that happen?"

"He was here, checking on Cassandra's dog. You know what? That doesn't matter. I need someone to find her for me, so I can go save her." He crossed his fingers.

"Right. I'll see what I can do. Just do whatever you have to do while you wait. He'll find you if he choose to help." She hung up without saying goodbye, but Nevan figured he kind of deserved her being rude. He was asking a big favor from her.

Most fallen tried to avoid Mika'il, the Warrior angel and the one in charge of them. He wasn't the most forgiving of creatures and requesting his presence to give aid to one of them was pushing the envelope of his tolerance.

His phone rang and after checking the ID, he answered, "Largent."

"Detective Largent, a package arrived here at the station for you. The man delivering it said it was urgent. Had to do with one of your cases," the desk sergeant told him.

"Thank you. Detective Davidson and I are our way back."

He hung up before heading to the car. Tommy climbed in then looked at him.

"We're heading back to the station?"

"Yes. There's a package for me. I'm assuming it's from the kidnappers and it'll help us get Cassandra back." He tore out of the driveway like he was being chased by hellhounds. And given how his day was going, he wouldn't have been surprised if he had been.

"You're not waiting for this Mika'il guy," Tommy inquired.

Nevan shook his head. "No. If he's going to help us, he'll find us."

"What is he? Some kind of black ops spook guy?"

"You could say that." Nevan wasn't about to get into Mika'il or Lucifer today. Neither one was worth his concern. It was all about Cassandra and getting her back safely.

Chapter Seven

"Wake up."

Cassandra gasped as cold water drenched her and she sat up, swinging. But they'd tied her hands and ankles together while she was out. She stilled, letting her senses work for her. She sat on the ground and from the sticks and stones poking her butt, she had to be in a forest. It had to be some park that had oak trees, since druids often had altars in clearings surrounded by them.

They were far enough away from the city that there was no sound of traffic or any other form of civilization. Unfortunately, they'd traveled while she was unconscious and she had no way of knowing which direction they'd gone or how long they'd driven.

"The detective has received the package and I'm sure he'll be contacting us directly."

The tone of that voice spoke of authority—he had to be in charge of the whole shebang. Yet there was also a timeless quality to his voice and she sent out her power to seek him. She bit back her gasp when her search revealed a soul with several lives tied to it. Whoever he was had been reincarnated hundreds of times over the centuries.

She slowly followed the strings and links between the souls, trying not to undo the delicate balance of lives. She wanted to find the first life that had started it all. Deeper and deeper Cassandra went until she found it. Protected behind a wall of other lives, it thrived and burned so brightly, she almost mistook it for a fallen. But a fallen wouldn't have died and been reborn. Once a fallen died, they went to wherever God had decided was best for them.

Now this one had the signature of a true druid. One of the original of that priestly class and one who did have actual magic. Not just the sight, like Nevan. This man had power and wasn't afraid to use it. Yet there was something broken with this soul as well. Like a piece of it was missing.

"Soon the moon will rise and the spells will be complete. Morgana and I will be reunited."

As she continued to study the soul, she started to absorb some of its memories. There was only one face connected to them and it was a red-haired woman dressed as a druid. She appeared through several of the lives, dressed differently but always the same woman. Until this most recent life, where there was a glaring absence of her touch.

"Can I have a coat or something?" Cassandra asked as she shivered, not just from the cold but also at the realization that this man believed he could bring Morgana back. Yet it wasn't a mistake that she hadn't been reborn in this lifetime. Something had happened the last time they'd been here and Morgana's soul no longer existed She wouldn't be coming back, no matter what the man did.

There was no magic in the world to bring those whose soul had died back to life.

"No. You should rejoice in being out in nature. You should be skyclad like the rest of us to worship our Mother."

Cassandra shook her head. "Sorry. This is as 'skyclad' as I'm going to get."

A phone rang and she laughed. "Great getting back to nature and the Goddess, guys. She doesn't like phones."

Of course, she never saw the slap coming. "You won't mock her. Your punishment will come soon enough."

Cassandra shook her head. "There is no punishment that can compare to what I've already gone through. You can do whatever you want to me. I've been through the worst pain imaginable. Torture means nothing to me."

"Losing your sight isn't a punishment. It's merely an obstacle to see how you react to it. If you're strong, you go on. If you're weak, you curl up and die." An older female voice hissed at her.

She laughed at them. "It's not my eyesight that was the pain. I had already lost heaven and my wings. The very meaning of my existence. What was eye sight to compare with that?"

"Heaven and wings? Are you trying to tell us you're an angel?" It was the one who'd been in her bedroom. Since he was there, she assumed his silent partner was as well.

"Yes, I'm a fallen angel." The point wasn't to get them to believe her or not. It was to buy time for Nevan to find her. She hoped Lucifer helped him and didn't try being a dick about things. "I was one of those foolish enough to rebel against God and because of my hubris, he banished me from heaven."

"Then whatever happens to you next is what you deserve," Leader said.

"Maybe, but to be honest, I'd rather take my chances on God's punishment than let you decide how I should be punished." She smirked.

"Sir, it's for you. It's Detective Largent."

So far, she'd determined there were at last five people there. Yet Patrick had been sure there were thirteen altogether in the cult. Cassandra would go on the assumption that all thirteen were there, waiting for the ritual to begin.

"Detective Largent, we have her and she's fine. Maybe a little cold, but it kind of chilly up here." Leader sounded so smug. "I'll text you directions where to meet one of my men. Remember no one can follow you."

Cassandra rested her forehead on her knees, praying for Nevan. It wasn't the first time she'd asked God to watch over mortals she loved, but it was the first time she knew that if Nevan died, she would be destroyed. Life wouldn't mean much if he wasn't there beside her.

"Is everything else in place? We will have to do the ritual as soon as he arrives. We can't give him time to rethink his decision. The moon will be at its highest pinnacle then." Leader's excitement began to show in his voice.

It was moments like this when Cassandra did miss her eyesight. If she could see, then she'd be able to make sure she could be a help to Nevan, not a hindrance.

"Suck it up, Cassandra. You've never pitied yourself in all the centuries you've lived. You've faced your problems

proudly and bravely. This is just another obstacle." Lucifer's words danced through her mind and she took courage in them. Whether anyone was coming to save her or not, she would find a way to escape.

She'd give up her own life for Nevan, so if it came down to that, she'd make the sacrifice.

It being dark and her not sure of where she was helped her lose track of time. She even dozed a little. The commotion of people moving brought her out of the chilly haze she was in.

"They're here."

"All right. Everyone, take your places in the circle."

Nevan stumbled. "You know if you'd take the bag off my head and stop shoving me along, I wouldn't be slowing us down. This is all your fault."

"Shut up."

He'd heard that particular order a hundred times since they'd grabbed him at the fountain where his cousin had been taken. He didn't plan on making it easy for them to deal with him. Whether he died or not, he wasn't going down without a fight.

A hard shove in the middle of his back sent him careening forward. Two sets of hands grabbed his arms then the hood was jerked off. He found himself standing in the middle of a stone circle, surrounded by ten naked figures. Only their faces were covered. He hid his horror at seeing some of those bodies. Cassandra was going to owe him big for making him have to see that.

"Detective Nevan Largent, do you know why you're here tonight?" The hooded man standing on a rock altar asked him.

"So you can sacrifice me for some kind of crazy ritual. You're trying to bring back some druid high priestess that I'm supposed to be related to." He didn't see the point in playing dumb. "You already tried it once with my cousin, but he lied and told you he had the gift. Bad for you, he didn't."

The priest frowned.

"Unlucky for me that I just happened to move here a while back. Should've stayed in Chicago, but after getting shot and having to deal with a city being overrun by fallen angels, I figured I'd have better time out here. Turns out California isn't all it's cracked up to be." He tried to find Cassandra amidst the shadows and people. "Before you get to bleeding me dry, I need to see Cassandra and make sure you didn't hurt her."

"I told you she wasn't injured. She's just cold." The man gestured toward the side of the altar and Nevan saw her seated at the edge of the stone platform. He could barely tell it was her in the flickering torch light.

"Man, this is the twenty-first century. Don't you think you could've used electric lanterns instead of torches? It's a bitch to see anything." His goal was to talk as much as possible while he worked on formulating a plan to get them out of there.

Rescue was coming. The idiot who nabbed him hadn't checked to see if he had a tracker on his clothes or anything, so the GPS device they'd stuck in his pocket was leading the police right to them, but Nevan didn't know how far out they were.

"Prepare him," the priest ordered.

Nevan fought with everything he could muster, yet odds were against him and soon he found himself stripped naked. They forced him to lie on the cold stone altar then strapped him down. His head hung off the end. To his amazement, he found himself staring into Cassandra's hazel eyes.

"Hey, honey," he whispered.

She startled, like she hadn't realized he was right there. "Nevan, why did you come?"

"I couldn't let anything happen to you. I told you I'd never let anyone hurt you again."

Cassandra smacked him on the back of the head. "Idiot. They can't kill me."

He laughed. "Sure they can. Not even a fallen angel can survive bleeding out, which is what it looks like they're going to do to me."

"I hope you brought back-up," she spoke softly.

"In theory, they should be en route. How close they are is an entirely different story."

She made a small noise that sounded like a sob.

"Don't cry, love. It'll be okay."

"I can't believe you can still say that while you're tied to a stone slab about to be sacrificed so some guy can try to bring back his wife who won't be coming back, no matter how many Largents he kills." Cassandra shivered.

Being this close to her, he noticed that she had on the T-shirt that she'd been wearing when he'd put her to bed that morning, and a pair of panties. That was it. "The bastards didn't even give you a chance to get dressed."

"Well, you know, kidnappers are inconsiderate that way. They don't give you a chance to get dressed, do your hair and make-up. To be honest, as kidnappers, these guys are pretty good." Her smile was a little wobbly, but he admired her ability to joke in the face of what was about to happen.

Then what she'd said a few minutes back hit him. "What do you mean, his wife isn't coming back?"

"Throughout time since they were druids in pre-Christian Ireland, their souls have been intertwined. When one was reborn, so was the other. They balanced each other and it kept him sane." Cassandra grimaced. "Unfortunately, something happened either in their last life together or at some point between then and now."

"What could've happened? Sounds like everything was running smoothly," he muttered.

Shrugging, she continued, "I don't know. He has no memory of it, which means he either wasn't there when it happened or he chose to forget it. But by not having that memory, he thinks that all he has to do is cast this spell and spill your blood and she'll come back to him."

"Oh man, this sucks. I might die for nothing. It doesn't get worse than that."

The tears trailing down her cheeks gleamed in the torchlight and Nevan knew there wasn't much he could say to help her. They were stuck having to wait for Tommy and the others. He was tied up and she was blind. "This is quite a predicament, isn't it?"

"Yeah." She hissed through her teeth. "Did you see Lucifer?"

"He's a complete jackass. I can't believe the two of you are friends. I couldn't get him to give me a straight answer until the last possible minute, then poof. He just disappeared."

He noted that the chanting had started and he caught the priest approaching the altar with a very sharp knife in his hand. In a way, he was glad that Cassandra couldn't see what was coming.

"That's Lucifer for you. Listen, if you were blamed for the fall and for every bad thing that ever happened in the world since people started keeping track, wouldn't you have an attitude?" She shrugged.

"Kaiser is fine. I think they just gave him some kind of drug."

The first slice across his stomach was quick and because the blade was so sharp, he didn't even realize the priest had done it until the pain hit him like being burned. He whimpered under his breath. He had to go as long as possible before saying anything.

He didn't want Cassandra to suffer hearing him begging like a coward, though he had a feeling that was coming.

"Those scars on your shoulder blades? Was that where your wings used to be?"

Another cut. This one on his left thigh.

"Yes. Mika'il cut them from me after I was banished from heaven." She reached to touch her back. "It's weird because sometimes even now I can feel them there. I go to touch them and cry when I realize they aren't there."

"Another reason for me not to like Mika'il." The next cut came across his right thigh.

She moved closer to him, resting her tied hands on his cheek. "Why wouldn't you like Mika'il?"

"Because I had Danielle contact him and tell him I needed his help. He never showed up."

"The archangel isn't at our beck and call, Nevan." She laughed, but he didn't hear any humor in it. "He might not have been allowed to come. There are times when I think Mika'il would help us if he could, but his orders are different and he isn't the kind to go against them."

Another cut. It was deeper than the others and across his wrist. He could feel the blood trickle across his skin to drip on the ground. This time he couldn't swallow the grunt.

"What's going on, Nevan?"

Cassandra lifted her head and he watched as she looked around her. He knew she was filtering through her senses to figure out what was happening. Surging to her feet, she dove at the priest, knocking him from the altar.

Nevan snorted. Obviously no one had seen that coming. There was chaos as people ran up to help get their priest away from the crazy blind lady who was kicking and scratching him. He didn't know how long it took them to finally corral her and tie her to the altar right next to his head again.

She leaned in to kiss him. "I'm sorry I couldn't help more."

"You delayed it another few minutes. That's all that Tommy needs to get here. I know he's coming, love."

He wasn't going to lose hope that the police would get there before he bled out. Cassandra kissed him then turned to look at the priest who was being helped to his feet.

"I want you to know that you can kill all the Largents in the world, but you are never going to get your wife back. She wasn't reborn in this life because her soul no longer exists."

"Shut up. You're lying." He slapped her and her head rebounded off the stone.

Closing her eyes, she seemed to be working through the pain and Nevan swore at the priest. "What kind of man are you that you're hitting a blind woman? I guess you're not much of a man, because she beat the shit out of you."

The priest glared at him, but Cassandra wasn't done with him. "What did you do? What kind of deal did you make that took her soul from her, but you got to keep yours? I know how it happens. I know how a soul ceases to exist and I want to know what kind of man bargains with the devil and makes his payment with his wife's soul."

Nevan shuddered. He grew lightheaded because the blood he was losing from all the cuts was adding up. "Come on, Tommy," he muttered. "You need to get here or we need a miracle of some kind."

"I made no such bargain. She is merely held by magic in the other world. We cast this spell and she will be free." The priest raised the knife, holding the point of the blade against Nevan's chest right over his heart. "A heart for a heart, and magic for magic."

"Seriously? I had hoped Mika'il would be able to come and save you, but apparently Mr High and Mighty has something better to do."

Nevan closed his eyes and groaned. If he was going to be saved by an angel, why couldn't it have been the archangel? He was going to hear about this for the rest of his life. He just knew it.

"Lucifer, what are you doing here?" Cassandra stared out into the middle of the circle where Lucifer stood, arms crossed and fingers tapping on his biceps. Nevan met Lucifer's eyes and for the first time, saw seriousness and determination in them. There wasn't any pain or anger. At least not yet.

The mortals dropped to their knees. All except for the priest. He still had the blade to Nevan's chest, though he studied Lucifer.

"We had a deal," he said.

Lucifer nodded. "Yes, we did, but it seems like you're trying to get back that which you gave away. Just like a mortal. Making deals and breaking promises. You made a deal with me for power and wealth and you paid your debt with your wife's soul."

He took a step toward the altar and Nevan gritted his teeth as the priest started to drive the point of the knife into Nevan's skin. Lucifer didn't seem interested in what was going on with Nevan. He stayed focused on the priest.

"I gave you all that you wanted, but still you want it all. You want the one true and real treasure you had back. Well, it's too late. She's mine now and you don't ever get that kind of love back." Lucifer took another step and the blade went another inch deeper.

Cassandra took his hand in hers, and though he knew he might end up breaking it, he held on. The pain radiating from his chest was excruciating. He wasn't sure how much longer he'd last before he passed out.

He shot Lucifer a glance, but this time there was rage swirling in those black eyes and disgust on his face.

"Like so many other mortals, you think you can have everything you want. You have only to ask and it will be given to you." Lucifer laughed and a woman screamed. "Such foolishness. You are a shining example of why I believed angels were superior to mortals in every way."

Another step, this time bigger and Lucifer was right at the edge of the altar. As he reached for him, the priest drove the knife into Nevan's chest. Fuck being brave. Nevan screamed in agony. As blackness began to take him, he found himself staring into a pair of silver eyes.

"Come with me for a little while. I'll return you when it's time."

He felt himself peel away from his physical form. Nevan started to look, but Mika'il touched his shoulder.

"I suggest you don't look. It isn't a pretty sight. Never was when Lucifer got angry."

"I can't believe he came to save us." He was pleasantly surprised, though he understood it was Cassandra, Lucifer was there to save. Saving him was a bonus for Nevan, and it probably didn't rate on Lucifer's chart of important things.

"Do you really think he was there to save you?" Mika'il shook his head. "He was there because the man was trying to take something he'd given Lucifer. Daystar doesn't give things back. Once he gets it, he keeps it."

Nevan strolled into a bright white room then turned to look at Mika'il, who went to sit at a large desk. "You truly don't believe he's anything but evil?"

"A leopard doesn't change its spots, Nevan. He's nice to people because it suits his purpose, not because he likes them or cares for them." Mika'il shuffled a pile of paper. "You can go out for a walk in the garden if you want."

"How long will I be here? And why am I here?"

"Call this your near-death experience and you'll be here until you're out of the woods. Now go somewhere. I have work to do."

Nevan stalked in the direction Mika'il had pointed. He kind of understood where the archangel was coming from, but he did think that Lucifer had done it because he cared for Cassandra and wanted her happy. He'd always believe that until the day he died a second time.

* * * *

Cassandra heard Nevan scream and knew whatever happened wasn't good. Before she could get free of her ropes, the police descended onto the clearing.

Tommy was there, cutting her loose and explaining what was wrong with Nevan.

While the other law enforcement rounded people up, Cassandra went with Nevan in the Medi flight that took him to Cedar-Sinai in Los Angeles. After changing into scrubs, she sat in the waiting room, hating the fact that no one would tell her anything.

Finally Eli arrived with Kaiser in tow and her own clothes to wear. She decided maybe she could call Danielle, because Nevan did consider the fallen a friend.

"Danielle Weston."

"Hello, Danielle. This is Cassandra Harmen. I wanted to let you know Nevan was critically injured tonight and he's in surgery."

"What hospital?"

"Cedar-Sinai."

"We'll be there ASAP. Hold down the fort, Cassandra. Help is coming."

"Thank you." Tears streamed down her cheeks. She accepted the tissue Eli handed her.

Danielle said, "We're all family. No matter how hard Nevan tried to push me away, I wasn't going to let him be out there without back-up."

Cassandra said goodbye, happy to know she wouldn't be alone for long. Nevan had friends and family who would be there to help her deal with everything.

So when Danielle and her husband arrived at the hospital the next day, Cassandra greeted them with hugs and a smile.

"Will he be all right?" Danielle asked as soon as they sat.

Cassandra nodded. "They're going to keep him unconscious for a few days to make sure he doesn't do anything to tear out the sutures and stuff like that. But they're giving him an optimistically fifty-fifty chance of making it. I think they're trying not to get our hopes up in case something does happen."

Danielle covered Cassandra's hand with hers. "Don't worry. Nevan is tough. He'll come out of it just fine and with another dashing scar he can make stories up about."

She laughed. "True."

And while they waited for Nevan to wake, they became fast friends as well.

Chapter Eight

"Nevan, wake up."

Nevan smiled, loving the sound of Cassandra's voice in his ear. He opened his eyes to grin at her. "Hey, love. I didn't know you were going stop by this early."

After sitting on the edge of the bed, she leaned over to kiss him. He savored the touch of her lips on his. *Christ!* He wished he was healthy enough to flip her on to the bed and have his wicked way with her. But the doctors said he couldn't have any strenuous activity for a few more weeks yet. When he didn't think he could take any more without begging for a blow job, he eased away from her.

"I always love your hello kisses," he said.

She giggled. "You say that about my goodbye kisses and good afternoon kisses and good morning ones."

"All right. I love all of your kisses whenever I can get them." He settled back against the pillows, wincing when the stitches in his chest pulled slightly.

"Are you okay?" She arranged his pillows then handed him his glass of water.

"Just sore. What else is new? I don't think that's going to change for a while yet."

"True."

He stared at her, thinking how close he'd come to losing his life and that if it hadn't been for Lucifer intervening, he would've died. Admittedly, it was touch and go there after the priest had plunged the knife into his chest, but Tommy and the police had gotten there in more than enough time to airlift him out of there.

When he'd come out of the medically induced coma, his parents, siblings, Cassandra and Danielle had surrounded him. The most important things in his life. His family, friends and the woman he loved.

He hadn't seen Lucifer or Mika'il since that moment and in a way, he was glad about that. He didn't like Lucifer and never would, but he did owe the fallen angel his life. Also, he disagreed with Mika'il about why Lucifer had shown up. They'd argued a few times until Nevan had realized he wouldn't ever change Mika'il's mind.

"Do you think Lucifer was there to save us or was he there to exact justice on the man who thought he could steal back what Lucifer rightfully bargained from him?"

Cassandra lifted one shoulder. "I would like to think that Lucifer's presence there was purely to help us. But I know better than that. He's not entirely misunderstood. He's done things that could be considered unforgivable. Yet he has a good heart and he does care about those who were his friends before the fall."

He took her hand. "And you were one of those?"

"Yes. We were friends long before he fueled the flames of rebellion. Almost as close as he and

Christian were." She smiled. "I know Danielle told you that Lucifer took Christian's soul."

"Yeah. She was crushed by that." He remembered hearing how sad she was.

"Good news. Christian reappeared a week or two ago after being gone for a month. He has no memory of what happened. He thought he was only gone for a week and had come out here to help us with our problem."

Nevan was happily astonished that Lucifer had let Christian return. "Maybe he's not all bad. Sometimes we sink to the low expectations people have for us."

"True." Cassandra lay down on the bed, making sure not to put any pressure on his chest.

They cuddled and she fell asleep. He sat there, stroking her hair and he remembered who he'd met while he was in the garden waiting for Mika'il to tell him he could go home.

He'd been sitting on a bench, enjoying the warm sunshine and the smell of the flowers. As he'd sat there, he'd noticed someone strolling along one of the paths. He'd never seen anyone else until that moment. After standing, he headed toward her.

She was a beautiful red-head and she smiled at him when he approached her.

"Hello," he said.

"Good day, sir." Her lilting Irish accent brought a matching smile to his face.

"I'm Nevan."

"I'm Morgana."

He bowed over her hand, then offered her his arm. "I haven't seen anyone else in the garden before."

"I'm new here. The black-eyed man told me I would be here for a few days or so until I decide whether to go back or go on. He says I have fulfilled the lessons I wanted to learn."

"He did, huh? Black-eyed man. He wouldn't happen to have a cross shaped brand on his left cheek, would he?"

"Aye. He was quite nice to me when I discovered what my husband had done." Tears welled in her green eyes. "I believed we would be together forever, but he chose power and money over love."

"Mortal men can be weak like that, Morgana. I'm sorry."

She looked at him. "But you aren't mortal, so what would you know about that?"

He chuckled. "Just because I'm wandering around this garden doesn't make me any more angelic than you."

Frowning, she studied him for a second then nodded. "It's all right. I'll believe for you."

He inclined his head. "Thank you for the faith."

They'd spent several hours together talking about the different worlds she'd lived through and the things she'd learned. He didn't know what her decision ended up being, since he'd had to leave before she'd made it. But he had made a new friend in a beautiful place and it had soothed his soul when he was missing Cassandra.

Before he'd left, Morgana had patted his hand and said, "Don't worry. You'll both be returning here when your time on earth has passed."

He shook his head. "I'm afraid not. My love has been denied entrance into heaven for her rebellion."

"Well, maybe by the time you come, she'll be forgiven." Morgana kissed his cheek then wandered away.

As he walked through the door from the garden into the waiting room, he suddenly found himself staring up into Cassandra's hazel eyes. He knew it didn't matter whether she went to heaven, hell or some place in between. He would always stay right by her side.

Closing his eyes, he fell asleep holding the person he loved most.

"You took his wife's soul as payment?"

Lucifer turned from the sight of Cassandra and Nevan wrapped in each other's arms. He met Mika'il's accusing glare with a little grin. "Of course I did. I get paid in souls, brother. What do I care whose soul it is?"

"Who was she? Where is she now?" Mika'il shook his head. "You're incapable of change, aren't you?"

"Her name is Morgana and she wanders the Garden of Eden, trying to decide if she will go to heaven or come back to earth in a new form to learn another lesson."

He smirked at Mika'il's stunned expression. "I took her soul to save her. I took her husband's soul to destroy him. There's a balance to that, Mika'il, and not even you can argue with that."

Mika'il turned away from Lucifer and as the fallen angel slowly faded, he held out his hand as if to touch Mika'il's shoulder. He disappeared before he could.

About the Author

I've been writing for most of my life, but was first published in 2004. I believe everyone deserves love in all its forms. I write about women and men who find strength in loving each other. I live in the Midwest with my two cats, and when I'm not writing (which isn't very often) I read and watch movies.

Tiffany Aaron loves to hear from readers. You can find her contact information, website details and author profile page at http://www.totallybound.com.

Totally Bound Publishing

Home of Erotic Romance